### *This couldn't be happening to Tally James, the girl whose prom date ran off with someone else.*

But it was happening, she thought, afraid to meet Jed's gaze, afraid of what she'd see in those dark, dangerous eyes.

"Relax, Tally," he said with a roguish smile. "There's nothing to be afraid of." His mouth was so close she could feel his warm breath fan her lips.

Then he kissed her. A mere brush of his lips across hers—tempting, tantalizing, making her want more.

Was this why she'd never married anyone else? Because she was waiting for Jed Whitmore to come back and marry her?

She was out of her mind. Jed Whitmore, while admittedly the sexiest man alive, was only using her to get what he wanted.

What about her? Would she marry to get what she wanted?

Dear Reader,

Silhouette Romance is celebrating the month of valentines with six very special love stories—and three brand-new miniseries you don't want to miss. *On Baby Patrol,* our BUNDLE OF JOY selection, by bestselling author Sharon De Vita, is book one of her wonderful series, LULLABIES AND LOVE, about a legendary cradle that brings love to three brothers who are officers of the law.

In *Granted: Big Sky Groom,* Carol Grace begins her sparkling new series, BEST-KEPT WISHES, in which three high school friends' prom-night wishes are finally about to be granted. Author Julianna Morris tells the delightful story of a handsome doctor whose life is turned topsy-turvy when he becomes the guardian of his orphaned niece in *Dr. Dad.* And in Cathleen Galitz's spirited tale, *100% Pure Cowboy,* a woman returns home from a mother-daughter bonding trip with the husband of her dreams.

Next is *Corporate Groom,* which starts Linda Varner's terrific new miniseries, THREE WEDDINGS AND A FAMILY, about long-lost relatives who find a family. And finally, in *With This Child...,* Sally Carleen tells the compelling story of a woman whose baby was switched at birth—and the single father who will do anything to keep his child.

I hope you enjoy all six of Silhouette Romance's love stories this month. And next month, in March, be sure to look for *The Princess Bride* by bestselling author Diana Palmer, which launches Silhouette Romance's new monthly promotional miniseries, VIRGIN BRIDES.

Regards,

Joan Marlow Golan
Senior Editor

Please address questions and book requests to:
Silhouette Reader Service
U.S.: 3010 Walden Ave., P.O. Box 1325, Buffalo, NY 14269
Canadian: P.O. Box 609, Fort Erie, Ont. L2A 5X3

# GRANTED: BIG SKY GROOM

## Carol Grace

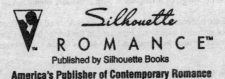

**Silhouette**

ROMANCE™

Published by Silhouette Books

America's Publisher of Contemporary Romance

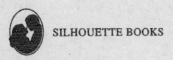

SILHOUETTE BOOKS

ISBN 0-373-19277-0

GRANTED: BIG SKY GROOM

**Printed in U.S.A.**

**Books by Carol Grace**

Silhouette Romance

*Make Room for Nanny* #690
*A Taste of Heaven* #751
*Home Is Where the Heart Is* #882
*Mail-Order Male* #955
*The Lady Wore Spurs* #1010
*Lonely Millionaire* #1057
*Almost A Husband* #1105
*Almost Married* #1142
*The Rancher and the Lost Bride* #1153
†*Granted: Big Sky Groom* #1277

*Miramar Inn
†Best-Kept Wishes

Silhouette Desire

*Wife for a Night* #1118

---

## CAROL GRACE

has always been interested in travel and living abroad.
She spent her junior year of college in France and toured
the world working on the hospital ship *HOPE*. She and
her husband spent the first year and a half of their marriage in Iran, where they both taught English. Then, with
their toddler daughter, they lived in Algeria for two
years.

Carol says that writing is another way of making her life
exciting. Her office is her mountaintop home, which
overlooks the Pacific Ocean and which she shares with
her inventor husband, their daughter, who is now twen-
ty-one years old and a senior in college, and their seven-
teen-year-old son.

## Tally's Wish List

1. A stable of Thoroughbred horses. (Purebred Arabians maybe or Morgans would be nice as long as I'm wishing.)

2. A ranch to keep them on, something on the order of White Horse Ranch. (Dream on—there's only one White Horse Ranch, and it belongs to Jed Whitmore.)

3. To be the best horse breeder and trainer in the whole state of Nevada. (Make that the whole country. Why not?)

4. The willpower to keep from falling in love with the one man whose heart I can't have—my husband's.

# Prologue

*What am I doing here?* Tally thought as she scanned the four other faces around the bonfire. Here it was, prom night in Harmony, Nevada, and she'd ended up at the after-prom beach party with Josh Gentry, the class president and football hero; his true love Molly; Jed Whitmore, the town bad boy who was more than a little bit drunk; and last but not least, Tally's warmhearted blond friend Suzy. There were barefoot girls dancing wildly down at the beach, guys skipping stones across the lake, couples wrapped in blankets behind the rocks, and music coming from a boom box. *How did I get here?* Tally asked herself.

Right after her date deserted her somewhere between the punch bowl and the dance floor, Tally knew it was going to be a terrible evening. She decided right then to go straight home after the dance, before anyone guessed the awful truth—that she was the only one there in a homemade dress.

But Suzy, in a rush to get to the beach party, dragged

her out the door of the high school gym and pushed her into the back seat of Josh's car where she was wedged in next to Jed, who was not just the baddest, but the richest and best-looking guy in town. The very same guy she'd had a secret crush on for the past four years. Her and every other girl in town. Tally's heart beat like a sledgehammer. She wanted to say something clever or sassy to him, anything at all, really, but she was tongue-tied and silent the whole way there.

Jed, who'd come to the dance at midnight straight from the local bar, planned to take his powerful new motorcycle to the beach. But Josh, acting mature and responsible as their class president, decided Jed was too drunk to drive and insisted he ride with them. And now, here they were, gathered around a hastily built bonfire, mired in awkward silence in the midst of laughter and music that swirled around them. Prom night at Harmony High was always followed by a big fun party at Lake Mariposa. But this group wasn't having any fun. Not yet, anyway.

"Great party," Jed said with a trace of sarcasm.

Tally nodded, looking around anxiously at the mismatched group. If only she could disappear into the crowd of noisy, laughing classmates, where her lack of social skills wouldn't be so obvious. Or better yet, if only she could giggle seductively and flirt with Jed the way other girls did. She might as well wish for the moon in the sky above. Because she wasn't the type.

"*Wonderful* party," Molly said dreamily, lacing her fingers through Josh's. That depends, Tally thought, on who you're with. With the right person, any party can be wonderful. Tally stifled a painful pang of jealousy. Not only did Molly have a boyfriend, she had a big family, a ranch and horses of her own, while Tally had none of the those things.

"Anybody want something to drink?" Jed asked in a slurred voice as he pulled a can of beer out of his jacket pocket. He looked around at the small silent group, a crooked smile creasing his handsome face.

"No, thanks."

"Not me."

Jed shrugged and tossed the can into the lake, where it landed with a splash. "Give it to the fish, then. I've had enough."

"You can say that again," Josh said. "You're sloshed out of your mind, and you missed a great dance."

"High school dances bore me. High school bores me," Jed said, not bothering to deny he'd been drinking. To show his disdain, he hadn't bothered to wear a suit; he was in his usual black jeans and leather jacket.

"What *doesn't* bore you?" Josh asked, more amused than irritated.

"Flying," he answered without hesitating.

"Is it true you're getting your own plane for graduation?" Tally asked with a sideways glance in his direction. She was surprised at herself. Getting up the nerve to speak to Jed Whitmore. It was no doubt because he'd come to the prom straight from the bar outside town and by tomorrow wouldn't remember anything that anyone said. Jed had always fascinated her from afar and on a few occasions, up close, too. His movie-star good looks had made her mouth go dry and her knees weak every time he looked her way. Which wasn't often.

Jed shrugged as if he didn't know or care what he got for graduation. But he cared. Even though he was inebriated, Tally could see the lines tighten around his mouth in the flickering firelight.

"Yeah, I'm getting a plane...a plane ticket to Boston," he said. "And college tuition at my father's school. It comes with complete instructions. What courses to take, what clubs to join and who to make friends with. Oh, yeah, especially the friends. It's not who you know, you know, it's what you...no... Oh, hell, you know what I mean." With that he closed his eyes and fell backward, his head hitting the sand with a thud.

Tally stared at him in surprise. Jed Whitmore had passed out before the party had even started. Or had he? While she watched, his eyes opened and he stared up at the stars, maybe dreaming of flying among the constellations, or maybe thinking of his domineering father who was trying to control his life.

"You'll get your plane someday," Josh assured him. "I wouldn't want to go to Boston, either, everything I need is right here." He squeezed Molly's hand.

"I envy you all," Suzy said, shaking her blond hair loose from the fancy French roll she'd worn to the prom. "Knowing exactly what you want."

Tally turned her head in her friend's direction. "You know what you want," she said reassuringly.

Suzy nodded. "Yeah, but how do you get a husband when all the good guys are taken or leaving town? Maybe I ought to move on. I don't want to leave, but I have no prospects. No boyfriend and no job."

"They're hiring at the feed and fuel," Tally suggested.

"I'm a town girl," Suzy reminded her. "What do I know about saddles and boots and feed sacks?"

"You could learn," Tally said.

"And think of all the men you'd meet," Molly suggested. "Every rancher from miles around buys his equipment at the store."

Suzy nodded thoughtfully.

"I'll teach you all you need to know about feed and fuel. You'll be a terrific saleswoman. You can't leave," Tally said anxiously. What would she do without Suzy to help her over the rough spots, like watching her parents' marriage fall apart as her father's business went downhill.

"Why would she leave this paradise?" Jed asked, sitting up to toss a stick at the fire and missing by a foot. "The town where nothing happens—except gossip, mucking out stables, and having everyone know everything about you. The best thing about Harmony is getting the hell away from it."

"Like in an airplane," Tally said, glancing sideways at him. "Isn't it scary?"

"I'll tell you what's scary," he said, gathering his thoughts with an effort. "That's staying in Harmony. I'd rather be buried alive. But flying..." Jed glanced up at the stars and wished with all his might he could leapfrog over the next four years. That he could be free of his father's influence and money. Free to be his own boss. "Flying is freedom, flying is seeing everything from a different point of view. Watching the town get smaller and smaller until the houses are just little boxes and then they finally disappear."

"Even yours?" Tally asked, in an awkward attempt at humor.

"Especially mine." By the look on her face, Jed knew she didn't understand. Nobody did. "From the air the whole ranch flattens out until it's nothing but squares of black and brown and green."

"And the people are all little ants, I suppose," said Josh.

"Damn right," Jed agreed, his voice ringing in his ears.

Tally sat up straight and stared at Jed in openmouthed surprise, realizing how drunk he must be to talk that way. "You don't know what you're saying. White Horse Ranch is the most beautiful ranch there is. If I had a place like that, I'd never leave."

"But it's not mine," he said, his brow furrowed, his tone morose. "It belongs to my dad. You don't know what it's like to work for your father. Once I get out of here, I'm never coming back."

Tally sucked in a ragged breath. Didn't know what it was like? She'd worked for her father in his hardware store ever since she was tall enough to reach the cash register. She didn't expect Jed to remember that. Why should he? But she knew exactly what it was like to work for your father. Unlike Jed, she was often stuck in the storeroom of the dusty hardware store, restocking screws, fasteners and nuts. "Never's a long time," Tally said primly, tucking an errant curl behind her ear.

"Hey," Josh said, as he lay on his back in his rented tux and looked at the sky. "A falling star."

"Make a wish, everybody," Molly said, lying next to him on the blanket.

There was a moment of silence while they all looked at the stars. The only sound was the crackling of the dry twigs on the fire. The crowd at the lakefront had drifted away and the music from the portable tape deck had faded in the distance.

"You go first, Jed," Molly said. "But we all know what you want. To get away from Harmony."

"Yeah, and then I want my own plane. Maybe more than one. And I want to make my own money. And to make my father—to show my father..."

Tally watched his face in the firelight, imagined she saw sadness in the depths of his eyes, but maybe that was just determination. She knew he'd do what he said. He'd leave Harmony, be a big success and never come back. A twinge of sadness hit her. She'd never known him, but now she would never get the chance.

High school was over. Everyone would go their own separate ways, scattering like dry weeds in the dry Nevada wind. The four years she once thought would never end had suddenly come to a complete halt and with them had ended any chance to ever know Jed Whitmore. Her lower lip trembled, and her eyes suddenly filled with tears of regret.

"Your turn," Jed said brusquely, turning to Tally. "What did you wish for?"

Tally stared into the flames, as if she needed time to think, but she didn't. She needed time to pull herself together. She knew what she wanted. She'd always known. "A horse of my own," she said at last. "A beautiful brood mare, with great lines. One to build a business on. Maybe even a ranch of my own." She lowered her head to cover her embarrassment. What must Jed think of Tally James, the daughter of the hardware store owner, having the audacity to wish for an expensive mare and a ranch of her own.

"That's just a dream," she assured him. "I'm on my own now. I've moved out and I've got a good job, working full-time at the Lazy Y. Room and board and a salary, too. The foreman's teaching me everything he knows about horses, then maybe someday..." The thought of actually living on a successful, working ranch brought a smile to her lips, and the possibility of raising horses for a living thrilled her more than anything anyone else was doing, including Jed.

"You'll get your ranch," Molly said kindly.

Tally sent her a grateful smile. "Maybe."

Josh sat up and braced his elbows on his blanket. "All I want is to have the kind of life my folks have, to marry the only girl I ever loved and the only girl I ever will love." He put his arm around Molly and hugged her to him and there was a collective "awwww" from the group around the fire.

Tally watched tears glisten in Molly's eyes at this touching declaration. How can he know, she wondered. How can they be so sure of anything? How she wished she could believe that love would last forever. Her parents' marriage had shown her that when hard times come, love dies. At least theirs had. As business dwindled at the store, her mother, feeling helpless, withdrew into a shell. Communication at home was meager, and Tally was glad to leave the apartment over the store and her parents seemed glad to have her go.

From the other side of the bonfire, Tally caught Jed's sardonic look when he heard Josh's wish. He doesn't believe in true love, either, or any kind of love, she thought. But with his looks and his money, it won't take long for some girl to talk him into it. She'd be a special girl, though. Someone who'd fit in with his life-style. Not some ordinary Harmony High graduate. Tally drew her gaze away from his handsome face, with the firelight reflected in his glazed blue eyes.

"What about you, Molly? What did you wish for?" Tally asked.

"I've got Josh and that's enough for me. But of course I'd like to win first place for my jam at the county fair some day," Molly confessed.

When Jed staggered to his feet and covered his face with his hands, Tally thought he was going to throw up, either from an overdose of alcohol before the dance or from Molly's sugar-sweet, homespun declaration.

What a bunch of small-town yokels, Jed thought, planting his black leather boots in the sand in an effort to stop the world from spinning around him and making him dizzy. Let them stay in Harmony. Like little ants on the ground. Babies and jam and horses were all they wanted. What was wrong with them? Take this Tally, for example. She could be something, do something besides ride horses. She was smart, sometimes even answering the questions in math class before the teacher asked them.

She wasn't pretty, she was too thin, all angles and straight lines. But he remembered somewhat hazily, how her rich chestnut hair had tumbled over her shoulders as she sat beside him in the car, how he'd been tempted to wrap her curls around his fingers to see if they felt as soft as they looked. Maybe she'd marry somebody with a ranch, he thought. Yeah, that's what she should do.

"What about you?" he asked, turning to her abruptly, and dropping his hands to his sides. "Aren't you going to get married, too?"

"Me?" Startled, Tally looked up as if she couldn't believe he was talking to her.

"Yeah, you. Do you ever think about anything but horses?"

"I might get married someday," she said casually. "But I like being on my own. Being able to support myself."

He nodded. He could understand that. Though he really knew nothing about her. He'd thought she lived in town. All he really knew was that her hair smelled like roses, and she was horse crazy. Oh, yes, and her date must have ditched her tonight.

"Don't wait too long to get married," Suzy advised.

"She's right, Tally," Molly said. "Or all the good men will be taken."

"I'll take my chances," Tally said, with a proud tilt of her chin. "It's not really that important."

"Tell you what," Jed drawled, as a brilliant thought penetrated the alcoholic fog that surrounded his brain. "if you're not married in fifteen years, I'll marry you."

A hush came over the group. Tally's mouth fell open in surprise. Her heart pounded erratically in her chest. Suzy giggled nervously. Molly and Josh looked at each other. Nobody spoke for a long moment. The ripples on the lake lapped against the shore. His words hung in the warm night air. *If you're not married in fifteen years, I'll marry you.* He was drunk. He didn't know what he was saying. Everyone knew that's why he said it.

"Well, what do you say?" he asked, his cynical blue gaze fastened on Tally, daring her to say yes, his mouth curved in a mocking half smile.

"You're not serious," she said when she finally could speak. "And you're not sober," she added under her breath.

"As if you'd be around in fifteen years," Josh said.

"Okay," Jed agreed. "*If* I come back and *if* we're both still unmarried, and if you can get away from your horse long enough, will you do it?" To his befuddled brain the idea was so sound and logical he didn't know why she didn't jump on it. Instead she was looking at him as if he was crazy.

Four heads swiveled in Tally's direction while they waited for her answer. Four pairs of eyes stared at her.

Awkwardly she stumbled to her feet and wrapped her arms around her waist, wishing she could still the rapid beating of her heart, wishing she could meet that electric

blue gaze of his and stare him down. Here he was, really
noticing her for the first time in her life, really looking
at her, and all she could do was stand there like a statue.
And wish he'd meant what he said. If he had, she'd be
laughing or crying or dancing around the campfire. Instead she had to pretend it was a big joke. "All right,
whatever you say. Fine," she said with a shrug. "but
it's never going to happen."

"Don't be too sure," Suzy murmured.

Molly stood and held her arms out wide while her
long white dress floated gracefully to the sandy beach.
"Come on, everybody, hold hands around the fire." For
a minute it looked like she'd be standing there, holding
on to thin air. Even Josh looked embarrassed. Jed was
trying to stay upright in the sand, while Tally was dis-
tracted and Suzy unsure. But finally, reluctantly, the others joined her.

Molly tilted her head back to look at the heavens, and
one by one the others followed her lead. Even Jed, the
eternal skeptic.

"Star light, star bright, first star we see tonight,"
Molly intoned. "Wish we may, wish we might, have the
wishes we wished tonight."

With that she squeezed the hands on either side of her
and, around the circle, after a brief awkward pause, everybody else did the same.

As Jed meandered drunkenly down the sandy path to
the car, he thought it was the stupidest thing he'd ever
done, wishing on a star with these naive Harmony kids.
No, even stupider was saying something about marrying
what's-her-name. It was all those beers he'd guzzled at
the Red Pump that had made him go a little crazy tonight, complaining about his father and talking about his
dreams and then saying whatever it was he'd said about

marriage to that girl from his math class. He shook his head and wondered if she'd agreed to whatever it was he'd said.

If she had, he ought to take it back now. Tell her he was just joking. But why bother? It didn't matter, because he was never going to see her again. He was leaving Harmony for good at the end of the summer, and he'd never be back. That was not a wish. That was a promise.

# *Chapter One*

There was nothing more beautiful on a spring morning than a field of Thoroughbred mares romping through the grass with their foals at their sides. So beautiful it brought tears to Tally's eyes. But were the tears for the poetry in motion on that grassy field or for something she couldn't have?

Whatever the reason, Tally James stopped her truck by the side of the road to watch the brood mares of the neighboring Plentywood Farm escort their young to the drinking trough. The dominant mare went first, followed by the others, with the most timid bringing up the rear. Tally smiled. If she were to choose just one mare for her own stable, she'd pick that first one, knowing how much the aggressive behavior of the dam could affect her foal.

But she didn't have a stable. She was renting White Horse Ranch from the Whitmores, and she couldn't afford a Thoroughbred mare of her own, as much as she wanted one. Stallions might be more glamorous, but

Tally knew that good brood mares were the foundation of a thriving horse ranch. The best mares dropped the best foals no matter who the stallion. It was the way they delivered, their personalities, even the quality of their milk that formed their offspring.

And of course there was imprint training, the human hands-on method that started when the foal was in utero. Tally was not only a firm believer in it, she'd become something of an expert in that corner of Nevada. Now if she could only try it on a horse of her own. But after fifteen years of working for others, boarding and training their horses, she was no closer to getting her own horses and her own ranch than she'd been when she graduated from high school with her big, unrealistic dreams.

She got out of her truck and went over to the fence, resting her chin on the top rail, her eyes on the horses silhouetted against the pale blue early-morning sky. As she watched, the mare she admired so much lifted her graceful neck, looked across the field and noticed Tally for the first time. Curious, the horse, whose name, Tally knew, was M'Lady loped across the grass, her foal at her side, heading straight for Tally.

The mare with her aristocratic long slim legs and lithe rangy frame stopped just short of the fence. Ears directed forward, nostrils dilated, the high-strung animal eyed Tally with interest, while her foal nuzzled her contentedly.

Climbing up onto the lower fence rail, Tally leaned over as far as she could and crooned softly. "Oh, you beautiful girl. Don't be afraid, M'Lady. I won't hurt you. I just want to say hello."

Curiosity overcoming her fear, the horse edged closer to sniff Tally's hand, then to lick her fingers with its rough sandpaper tongue. Tally breathed a sigh, then oh, so gently ran her hand over the mare's smooth neck, admiring the long, flat muscles, like those of a long-distance runner.

"What wouldn't I give to have a horse like you," Tally murmured. "Would you like to come home with me?"

The horse raised her head and Tally, with her vivid imagination, could have sworn she nodded. "The problem is I can't afford you," Tally explained earnestly, rubbing the mare's forehead. "I can't even afford a pony of my own yet, let alone a gorgeous Thoroughbred with your credentials. But someday...one of these days," she promised herself.

Now that her mother had remarried, she *could* start saving for the things she wanted most. Horses of her own, a place of her own. Maybe even White Horse Ranch, if it ever came up for sale. If she was going to dream, why not dream big? She just had to work a little harder to make her dreams come true. Give more riding lessons, board more horses, do more imprint training...and win the lottery.

And not waste time coveting other people's horses when she had so much work to do at the ranch. Reluctantly she said goodbye to the sleek mare and her leggy, ungainly baby, got into her truck and drove away. But in the rearview mirror she saw the mare and foal still at the fence, and in her heart she felt a painful longing for everything she didn't have, couldn't have and maybe never would have.

The next Saturday Tally was in town as usual to pick up supplies and, as usual, took time out to have coffee with her friend Suzy. The diner was always noisy and crowded on weekend mornings in Harmony. Ranchers and cowboys washed down stacks of pancakes with mugs of strong coffee at the counter, while the tables were filled with families eating home-made biscuits and gravy. Tally, sipping her coffee in a vinyl booth near the door, leaned forward and regarded her best friend with curiosity.

"Well, what's the big news you couldn't tell me over the phone?"

Suzy's violet eyes sparkled with excitement. "Guess who's back in town?" she asked. "Jed Whitmore," she announced without waiting for an answer. "And he flew in on his own plane."

Tally set her cup down with a thud. "But why? Why would he come back now, after all these years?" she asked.

"Maybe he's back for our reunion," Suzy said.

Tally shook her head. "Jed Whitmore back for a high school reunion when he couldn't be bothered to even come to the prom until it was almost over? You haven't forgotten that he thought he was too good for Harmony, have you?"

"Of course not. But people change. Look at our classmates, most of them married with kids and twenty-five pounds overweight. Some of us are single parents like me and like Josh Gentry. Then there's you. You've turned into the premier horse breeder and trainer in the county. But that's no surprise. You always had a way with horses."

A way with horses, yes, Tally thought, but not with men. Suzy, on the other hand, had gone through a dozen boyfriends since high school and a dozen jobs. Now Suzy had a darling baby boy but still no husband and no steady job.

"So you think Jed has changed," Tally said lightly.

"Sure, but I don't know how he could have gotten any better looking," Suzy said with a sigh.

"Maybe he hasn't. Maybe he's lost all his hair and he's fifty pounds overweight," Tally suggested.

"That I have to see," Suzy said with a giggle. "And when I do see him, I'll ask him why he's here. Could be he's got some unfinished business to take care of. Loose ends, if you know what I mean." Suzy gave her friend a meaningful glance, which Tally chose to ignore. As soon as she could she changed the subject, paid the bill and headed for the feed and fuel store just as she did every week. But today her stomach churned and her pulse raced.

Just yesterday, as she was feeding the horses, a small plane approached the ranch from behind the house, banked left, turned and shot past her. Tally seethed with anger, fearful for herself and for the horses as the plane circled above her. Over the wing she caught a glimpse of a face in the cockpit, hidden behind aviator sunglasses. She should have known—she should have guessed it was him—but she was suddenly blinded by the propellers flashing in the early-morning sunlight. The noise was deafening, ten times louder than anything she'd ever heard.

Tally shook her fist at the plane as the horses reared and bolted in fear. After one more turn, he finally flew off into the sky, leaving her to calm herself and her nervous horses.

As she drove down the long, straight ribbon of highway back to the ranch, Tally was convinced it was Jed who'd buzzed the ranch yesterday. She tried to remember the last time Jed had been back in Harmony, but couldn't. She doubted he considered it home anymore, though the ranch was in his name, since his father had left it to him in his will.

His name was on the rent checks she wrote every month and deposited in his account at the bank. He was an absentee landlord in the best sense of the word. Absent everywhere but in her dreams. Tally had been troubled by dreams of Jed Whitmore since she was a teenager. There was nothing strange about that. Probably every girl in town dreamed about him at one time or another. But they'd doubtless gotten over it. Gotten over *him.*

But she hadn't. Even knowing he'd never thought about her, never even answered the letters she wrote about the upkeep of the ranch. On the other hand he never bothered her and never raised the rent. She should be grateful. She *was* grateful.

Outside of owning her own place, renting from the Whitmores with their hands-off attitude was the best possible situation she could hope for. And one of these days she'd stop dreaming about him. As soon as she found somebody else with charisma, good looks, money...

The thought of Jed coming back to Harmony to possibly upset her life caused a tremor of fear to shimmy down her spine. But Jed hated Harmony, she reminded herself. Wasn't interested in the ranch. Or her. Then why return at all? Why make a dramatic entrance, buzzing her without notice? If he had to come back, why not drive over in a car like anyone else? Because Jed never did anything like anyone else. She knew that—just as she knew, in a sudden flash of intuition, that he'd be waiting for her when she got home. Before she was ready. Before she'd had a chance to mow the weedy back pasture or to mend the fence. Or prepare herself mentally to see him again.

He was leaning casually against the gnarled oak tree that had been there as long as the Whitmores had owned White Horse Ranch. All six-foot-three, sun-bronzed, rich-beyond-belief, bad-boy rebel rolled into one gorgeous sexy package. She sat in her truck, gripping the steering wheel, wishing he hadn't seen her, so she could drive away and pretend he wasn't there.

"Hi," he called. His trademark brilliant blue eyes observed her coolly.

Tally got out of her truck slowly, reluctantly, glancing around for a glimpse of his Beechcraft, Piper Cub or whatever his plane was called, willing her knees to stop knocking, sure this was not a social call. Any more than the last one was. She and Jed Whitmore didn't move in the same social circles. She didn't move in any social circles. She didn't have time. She rode, trained, fed, boarded and showed horses. She worked from sunup to sundown and then some. Jed Whitmore didn't have to work.

"Are you looking for me?" she asked. At second glance he was even better looking than she remembered. If you liked sun-streaked brown hair that brushed his blue denim collar, a strong, muscular body, and a face that showed his wealthy upbringing. Stop, she told herself. He was just a man. But what a man. His face had only improved by the addition of laugh lines at the corners of his eyes. But he wasn't laughing now.

He ambled toward her, letting his gaze roam from her tousled hair to the tips of her old scuffed boots. Self-consciously she glanced down at her smudged plaid shirt, tugged at the knot of hair at the nape of her neck, and wished she'd dressed for the occasion. But what *was* the occasion?

"I'm looking for the James who rents this place," he explained, surveying her through narrowed eyes.

He didn't remember her, she realized with a sharp pang of disappointment. Had no idea who she was... while she remembered every word he'd ever said to her. But then, there hadn't been that many over the years.

"That's me," she said. "Tally James. And I'm looking for the pilot who buzzed the ranch yesterday, spooked the horses and every other animal within two miles."

"Sorry," he said. "I wanted to see the ranch."

"You could have warned me."

"*Natalie* James," he said abruptly, snapping his fingers. "The girl who loves horses, right? *You're* leasing my land?"

Hearing the surprise in his voice, she squared her shoulders and took a deep breath. So he remembered her. "Yes, I am. I thought you knew. We have a rental agreement."

"I'm sure we do. But I've lost touch these past years. Why don't you bring me up-to-date?"

What did it mean, up-to-date, Tally wondered. Up-to-date on the ranch, the community, the high school crowd or her personally? She told herself it was anything but the latter. Why would Jed Whitmore be interested in what had happened to her?

"Yeah. What's happened around here?"

Tally decided that "around here" must mean Harmony, so she took a deep breath and began to bring him up-to-date.

"Well, the Bettmans next door sold out to a developer and moved to California."

"I heard about that," he said. "Is that all in fifteen years?"

"Of course not. Did you hear that Mr. Snavely, the school principal, got a divorce and a toupee and married Miss Barkely, the church organist?"

"Old Snavely with a toupee?" Jed asked. "I spent more time in his office than I did in class, staring at his bald head and listening to him lecture me."

Tally smiled at the picture of Jed slouching in a chair in front of the principal's desk. "I remember."

"And I remember you, Goody Two-Shoes. You came into the office and delivered the absence slips. What's happened to you since then?" he asked, approaching the truck where she stood holding on to the door handle as if she might need to escape from him.

"Nothing," she said, relieved to see him stop a few feet away. "I'm just the same, no divorce, no toupee."

"Wrong," he said. "You're not the same at all. I wouldn't have recognized you. You've changed." Again that long lazy appreciative look that probably made every woman who crossed his path feel faint.

"Really?" she said. "You haven't." Wild horses couldn't drag the truth from her. That he'd only gotten better looking. "I guess you'd like to look around," she said.

"I already did." He stuffed his hands in his back pockets. "What in the hell have you done to the place? Nothing, as far as I can see."

She felt the heat of embarrassment flood her cheeks. All the time he was asking questions, telling her to bring him up-to-date, he meant with the ranch, not the town, and definitely not her. "If I'd known you were coming..." she stammered.

"Yeah? What would you have done, fixed the fences, reroofed the barn, painted the house? It's called up-keep."

Tally leaned back against her truck for support. "I know what it's called and I know what needs to be done. I wrote you about it, but—"

"But what? I thought I had someone here who was capable of keeping the place up, who was self-sufficient. Instead I've got...*you?*" He looked at her as if she was only a little above a horse fly, instead of a seasoned horse trainer.

"Look," she said, "I didn't want to make major repairs without getting your permission. So I sent you some estimates on fixing the ranch house, repairing the barn and putting in a new irrigation system. But I never heard from you."

"I've been on the go. The mail stacks up. I've got other things on my mind," he explained.

"The only thing on my mind is the ranch. Maybe it doesn't look like it used to, I'm sorry about that, but I don't think it's my fault. I actually know more about running a stable and training horses than most people in this county. I do imprint training, and I've earned my share of ribbons. Have you seen the horses?"

"From a distance, which is close enough for me."

"You don't like horses?" she asked incredulously.

He shrugged. "What's there to like? Four legs, a mane, a tail and a brain the size of a walnut. I'd rather see the facilities."

"This way then," she said raising puffs of red Nevada dust as she strode down the path toward the pasture where the mares and colts whinnied their greetings.

Tally had no intention of apologizing for the way the place looked. Not to someone who didn't even like horses. She knew what was expected of a tenant. And what wasn't. She had no money to spend on other people's repair problems. When he tore into her, it made her hackles rise. And caused her to brag about her talents. As if he cared about her blue ribbons.

Her cheeks reddened, thinking of what she'd said, how she'd talked about herself, when all he seemed to care about was the run-down condition of the ranch. He certainly didn't care that he'd frightened her and her horses the day before, or that she'd made an effort to get in touch with him over the past year. But the sight of the pale palominos, the spotted pintos and the hardy Arabians in the corral almost made her forget the ill-tempered owner of this land...until he stopped next to her and rested his arms on the top of the fence next to her and she was acutely aware of his masculine presence. Of the scent of his expensive aftershave.

Trying to ignore him, she offered the horses carrots from her shoulder bag, greeting and speaking softly to each one in turn. The sun warmed her back and shoulders. The smell of hay and horses filled the summer air. She'd almost relaxed when Jed's arm brushed against hers. She jerked away as if he'd touched her with an electric cattle prod.

"This is the largest corral," she explained.

"Uh-huh. These horses all yours?"

"They're all boarders. I don't have any horses of my own. Not yet. But they feel like mine because I've trained them all and shown them. And they're easily frightened by loud noises," she said pointedly.

"I said I was sorry. Seeing the place from the air is important. One thing I noticed was the broken fences.

Like that.'' He pointed to a splintered board on the other side of the corral.

She glared at him. As if she hadn't noticed. As if you needed to have a plane to see broken fence. The man is gone for some fifteen years, and he has the nerve to drop in on her without warning and start criticizing. Not that there wasn't room for criticism. "I know about the broken fence. In fact I have the fencing in my truck. So if you'll excuse me..."

"I'll give you a hand."

She looked at the creases in his designer jeans, at his expensive boots.

He caught her disparaging look. "You don't think much of me, do you?" he asked. "But I do function in the real world. I also fix fences. Maybe you think you don't need help, but the ranch is falling apart and you've let it happen on your watch."

"On my watch? I'm a rancher, not a sea captain," she said, aware of how strident her voice sounded. What was it about this man that brought out the worst in her?

"Well, I'm a pilot, but I know something about ranching. I grew up here, you know."

She crossed her arms over her chest. "Yes, I know. I also know that you couldn't wait to leave this place. That you had no interest in Harmony or the town or your family, either. In the five years I've been renting the place, I never heard one word from you. You never answered one of my letters. I could have been operating an...an ostrich farm here for all you care."

He stared at her, stifling an impulse to laugh out loud. Where did *that* come from? Where did this spitfire come from? This couldn't be the same shy Tally James from Harmony High, could it? The skinny, horse-crazy kid he used to see mucking out stables in return for riding privileges at every ranch within fifty miles?

Was this the same girl who sat in front of him in math
class his senior year who'd miraculously turned into a
woman with flashing silver-gray eyes, flushed cheeks
and an unruly mane of chestnut hair? He took a step
forward to get a closer look. Flushing under his scrutiny,
she turned on her heel and started toward her truck.

"Hey," he said, following close behind her. "What
is it with you? What did I do except offer to help you
with the fencing?"

"You criticized the way I've run the ranch."

"What did you expect, that I'd give you another blue
ribbon and a pat on the back?" He looked at her back
and then at her firm bottom and long legs poured into
well-worn jeans. At the mane of silky curls that tumbled
over her shoulders.

The scent of her shampoo that wafted back in his direction propelled him back fifteen years to calculus class.
He remembered trying to concentrate on equations while
her hair brushed the back of her chair and teased his
senses. Yes, it was her all right. But just to be sure, he
continued to look at her when she wasn't looking, as
they worked together on the fence in stiff, uncomfortable
silence. Measuring, sawing and hammering. And occasionally muttering.

"Hand me that post."

"Give me the hammer."

"Got any more wire?"

After he drove the last nail into the post, he stood and
wiped the sweat from his forehead with a white monogrammed handkerchief. "So," he said. "What will you
do when your lease is up?"

Tally straightened from where she was kneeling on

the ground. "I thought I'd renew. I always have, I mean...why do you ask?"

"I'm putting the place on the market."

"What...why?"

"I need the money."

"But...what about me?"

"You'll have to move."

"I don't want to."

"So buy it from me."

She bit her lower lip to keep it from trembling. She told herself not to let him see how upset she was. How much she loved it there. "How much do you want for it?"

She had guts, he'd have to admit that. She also had delusions of grandeur. "More than you can afford. And now that I've seen the condition it's in, I don't know what to do."

"How much?" she repeated.

"For you? Two and a half million. Cash."

He heard her gasp of surprise. "Why?"

"Why?" He grinned. "Because I like you."

He noted that when she blushed again, her cheeks were tinted scarlet as a Nevada sunset. And the flush extended right down the vee of her flannel shirt and beyond.

She caught his gaze and hastily fastened the top two buttons on her shirt. "I mean why are you selling?"

"I told you, I need the money," he said, bringing his gaze to meet hers.

"But I thought you were rich."

"Yeah, well it's all relative. You need money to make money, and my money's all tied up. I'm counting on the ranch." Counting on it coming through for him now. Until he'd seen it. The disappointment welled up in his throat and threatened to choke him. Okay, he'd neglected the place. Almost forgotten about it. But why couldn't she have told him it was falling apart?

"So you couldn't get in touch with me," he said. "Why didn't you tell my mother what was happening?"

"I did. But she said it was your ranch, and she gave me your E-mail address. Apparently you never got that message, either."

He shook his head and looked around at the sprawling house in the distance, flanked by old trees, vines not quite covering the peeling paint, at the sagging roof, and he clenched his jaw to stifle his frustration. Maybe she had tried. Maybe it was his fault for moving around so much, for ignoring his mail. For not selling it years ago when it was in its prime.

But he was waiting until he needed the money. And he needed it now. Desperately. His partner in their small commuter airline had to sell and Jed wanted to buy him out. When Jed owned the whole thing he'd be free to run it the way it should be run. He'd change the routes. Take it to towns where the bus had quit going and people were isolated. He'd go after the mail contract. He was bursting with ideas. Impatient to get going.

A pale palomino, its ears flicking back and forth, leaned over the fence and nudged him inquisitively. Without thinking he reached up to scratch its neck while his mind raced.

"Marshall Thompson still the bank president?" he asked, suddenly seeing a glimmer of hope.

Tally watched Gypsy bring her ears forward and gaze at Jed with a soft, adoring expression in her eyes. What was wrong with Gypsy? Didn't she know he was the town playboy? He hadn't lost his charm, with horses anyway. And if he didn't like them, you couldn't prove it by Gypsy.

"What? Oh, no. His son Dwight took over. You know Dwight, short and stocky with glasses, he was in our class."

"Yeah, that's right. We had a great class, didn't we. Lots of spirit."

"I'm surprised you remember. You weren't exactly Mr. Class Spirit."

"No, I left that for Josh Gentry. But I remember certain things, like that night of the prom."

"The one you came late to."

"And certain people. You for example. You said you wanted a horse and you thought I was crazy for leaving White Horse Ranch."

"I *love* White Horse Ranch. If I had the money…"

Jed looked around again. He would have liked to have seen a spotless stable sporting a fresh coat of white paint and tubs of bright flowers the way it used to be. On the other hand the place was basically clean and the horses were obviously well loved and well cared for. No, she didn't have the money, and neither did he. But maybe between the two of them…

"What do you say we go see our old pal Dwight?" he said as they walked back toward the house.

"We?" She stopped suddenly and stared at him, her gray eyes wide with surprise. "What for?"

"To ask for a loan. I'll put the ranch up as collateral. I'll hire you to be my foreman, I mean woman, manager, whatever. Then when we get the place fixed up…"

"You'll sell it for two and half million."

"You have a problem with that?" he asked. "I'll make it worth your while."

"Do you ever think about anything but money?"

At that moment he was thinking about looking her up in the yearbook, just to see how much she'd changed. And she had changed. Because if she'd looked then the way she looked now he wouldn't have stayed away so long. The wide-set eyes, the soft lips, the full breasts under the baggy shirt made him want to see more, to know more about her. Where had she been all these years besides his ranch?

"Everybody needs money," he said propelling her forward with his hand on her elbow toward the grove of trees where he'd parked his sports car. "You need it and I need it, too."

"Yes, but..."

"Bank open today?"

"It's Saturday. Besides I can't go back to town. I was just there. I've got lessons all afternoon, equipment to repair..."

"Don't forget the imprint training," he said. "That can really eat into your day."

Tally narrowed her eyes. "Do you know *anything* about horses?"

"I know what's important. I heard enough horse talk when I lived here. High spirit, firm muscles, steady gaze. Elegance, excitement and lots of energy."

The way he was looking at her raised goose bumps on Tally's skin. Was he talking about horses or was he talking about women, too? And if so, did she measure up? Not that it mattered. He was the richest man in town. She was the poorest woman. Out of the corner of her eye she noted his vintage Porsche parked under the trees. Reminding her of his wealth. Of the gap between them. As if she'd forgotten.

The lines at the corners of his eyes deepened, as if he was laughing at her. Under the tree in the mottled sunlight his hair gleamed gold. He ignored the car door and gracefully jumped over it into his car seat.

"I thought you flew in," Tally said.

"I did but I had my car delivered here after the engine was rebuilt. These roads are the few places left you can go 120 without anyone bothering you."

"Oh, really," she said, thinking of Sheriff Dowling sitting behind the wheel of his unmarked patrol car at the crossroads waiting for speeders like Jed.

"Really. You'll have to come with me some time," he said over the roar of the engine, reminding her of another summer day a long time ago—the last time he'd invited her to go riding with him. He had been roaring down Main Street on his motorcycle. Her father and all the other merchants were peering out of their shop windows, frowning with disapproval. Tally, standing on the curb, watched mesmerized as he screeched to a stop and beckoned to her to hop on behind him.

She looked around. *Her?* Did he mean her, Natalie James, the girl who wore second-hand clothes to high school, worked for her father after school and never dated?

"Get on," he yelled over the roar of the motorcycle's powerful engine.

She still didn't know how she'd had the nerve to do it. It was as if he had some strange power over her that she couldn't resist. Whatever it was, she jumped on the back of that motorcycle, as if she did it every day of her life, wrapped her arms around his waist and took off. The ride lasted all of three minutes. That's how long it took to go around the block.

She still remembered the noise, the vibration of the motor, her breasts pressed against his back and the smell of his leather jacket. It was over almost before it began.

He stopped just long enough for her to get off to face her angry father, then Jed sped away, and he never offered her another ride or mentioned it again. Neither did she.

"Or I'll take you up in the air," Jed said, jerking her out of her reverie.

"I've never been up in a small plane," she said. She'd never been up in a big plane, either. And she had no intention of going up in the sky in either one. Not with her acrophobia. But she didn't want to admit that to a jet-setter. She shielded her eyes from the sun's reflection in the polished surface of the Porsche.

"Thirty-two years old and you've never been up in a small plane?"

"How do you know I'm thirty-two?" She ran her hand through her hair self-consciously. "I guess I look it."

"You don't look a day over thirty-one," he said with a disarming grin. And then with a throb of his high-performance engine, and a spinning of the mag wheels, he was gone. Without another word about the loan, the bank, her rent or her future. Or the offer he'd made fifteen years ago.

Tally blamed herself for not asking about the loan or the bank or her rent. For standing there staring at him. For getting lost in her memories and in his brilliant blue eyes. For watching the clouds of dust on the horizon long after he'd gone.

She forced herself to go through the motions all afternoon. To give lessons to seven kids and three adults. To supervise the teenagers who mucked out the stables for her as she had once done for other owners. To confer with the paid help, the two stable hands who worked for her. And to work with the foals, doing imprint training.

And every minute she thought about Jed Whitmore, remembering how his criticism stung, how his elbow brushed hers making her heart beat double-time. And how his mood had changed when he figured a way out of his dilemma.

Lord, he was maddening. He positively oozed wealth and breeding. He'd always been too good-looking for his own good. What did he know about work that "ate" into your day? What did he know about work, period? Though she had to admit, he wasn't bad at fence repair. The work had gone twice as fast with him helping her. And those muscles, the ones that rippled under his denim shirt as he hammered. Those kind of pectorals didn't come out of a cereal box.

It was hard to keep her mind on the horses, as much as she loved the animals, when her whole future was up in the air. If he sold the place, where would she go? Where could she afford to go besides a room in town, like the rooms she'd grown up in above her father's hardware store. Where would she train horses or give lessons? Would she go back to being a stable hand at somebody else's ranch? In one day she'd gone from feeling like the master of her own domain to being at the mercy of a rich landlord. It was a horrible feeling. And it was Jed Whitmore's fault that her world was falling apart.

Jed had his own set of questions to answer on his way back to town. How long would it take to get the ranch in shape? How much money would he need? And last but not least, how was he going to talk Tally James into overseeing what had to be done? True, she had no visible alternatives, but there was that stubborn streak evident in the set of her chin, and in the look in her eyes that worried him. Did she really think she could buy White Horse Ranch? What kind of a crazy dream was that?

When he parked in front of his mother's spacious town house, he remembered it was her bridge club day, and he detoured around the back and let himself in through the kitchen. But when the wind blew the back door shut and gave him away, his mother called him.

"I want you to meet my friends," she said, putting her cards down as he appeared in the door to the high-ceilinged living room.

They beamed at him, they asked a million questions, and it wasn't until they'd left an hour later that he could ask his own questions.

"What's the story on Tally James?" he asked leaning against the refrigerator and cramming a leftover tea cake into his mouth.

His mother smiled indulgently as she poured him a glass of iced tea. "She's a remarkable girl, your tenant. Did you see her? She hasn't changed a bit, has she?"

"I noticed some…changes." Remarkable changes. She was no longer shy or uncertain. She was comfortable with who she was, proud of her accomplishments, at home on his ranch. It made him realize that he wasn't that much at home anywhere. Not at his condo in San Francisco nor his town house in Reno. Which was neither here nor there.

"Such a lovely girl and after all she's been through…"

"What? What has she been through?"

"That ugly mess with her father. I thought you knew."

"No."

"While you were away, he lost the hardware store when the big discount chain came in down the highway.

They offered him a job, but he turned it down. No one blamed him for that. I mean how could he work for someone else when he'd been his own boss for so long? He refused to give up, keeping the store open for the few faithful customers who stayed loyal. Running it at a loss until the bank took over the whole place including the apartment upstairs where the family lived. They found him in the garage the day before they had to move out, dead of exhaust fumes. It was ruled a suicide so they didn't even get to collect the insurance. And then her mother… Well, you know.''

"No, I don't know," he said impatiently.

"That's right, you were in Reno then. Well, Tally's mother had barely buried Sid before she left town. She just couldn't face anyone in Harmony. She went to Vegas to get a job in the casinos. But Marge was never a strong person, and didn't have the nerves for that kind of thing. So Tally's been supporting her all these years.''

"How?" Jed asked.

"Lessons, training, breeding horses for others. She's very good at what she does, and in demand all over. But still…it must have been a strain on her finances. But there's a happy ending. She just got married, I hear.''

"Who, Tally?" he asked, startled.

"No, her mother. Tally's never married. And she's so attractive. But there's really no one around. And she's been working so hard.''

So Tally had been supporting both herself and her mother. Why hadn't someone told him? "Do you know where my old yearbooks are?" Jed asked.

"Somewhere," she assured him. "I got them out when Darlene Allen called about your fifteenth class reunion. She was just delighted when I told her you'd be here for it.''

He shuddered at the thought of a sea of vaguely familiar faces, crepe paper streamers, overweight, twice-married classmates and watery punch. "My plans are up in the air. I don't know where I'll be."

"But I promised her. They're going all out this year. You can't let them down."

Jed took a large gulp of tea. "I may stay around awhile. Or I may not. The ranch needs some work."

"You're going to work on the ranch?" she asked incredulously. "Your father would be so pleased. He always hoped you'd come back to Harmony one day and live at White Horse. He loved it so much. That's why he left it to you." She sighed. "But you always had a mind of your own. He respected that."

*Respected it but disapproved of it.* His father wanted a carbon copy of himself, and Jed could only be Jed. He'd had a hard enough time finding out who that was. For years he turned his back on his father and his father's efforts to bring him into the family business ventures, whether it was mining or land development—until he realized working for his father was one way to get enough money to buy the plane he'd always wanted. Surprising his father and himself by his aptitude for buying and selling land, he had taken the money he made, bought his plane and quit the business.

His father didn't live to see him start the airline. Jed liked to think his dad would have been proud to see him succeed on his own, would have encouraged him to buy out his partner. But he wouldn't have approved of him selling the ranch, so he was just as glad his father wasn't there to tell him what to do. He knew what he had to do. As soon as he got the money from the ranch, he'd have the airline to himself at last.

"I'd stay only long enough to get the place into

shape,'' Jed warned. ''Harmony is not really my kind of town.''

''What is?'' she asked, her forehead creased with faint worry lines.

''Good question,'' he admitted. ''The only place I feel at home is up in the air. I'd have to say I haven't really found a place I'd want to live the rest of my life. But I'm going to get the ranch back to the way it was, providing that the bank will lend me the money for the repairs.''

''Of course they'll lend you the money. Your father helped found that bank along with Marshall Thompson. And if you're still here you can ride a palomino in the Fourth of July Parade,'' she said. ''Much safer than flying around in the sky in that little plane of yours.''

Jed let that remark go by without voicing his aversion to horseback riding. No point in upsetting his mother. Or in quoting statistics about the dangers of accidents in the air compared to accidents on the ground. ''If anyone rides a palomino in the parade, it should be Tally James,'' he said. ''She'd be good at it.'' She'd look good, too, he thought, with her proud bearing, her carriage and her easy manner.

''She does have a way with horses. Everyone says so. Have you heard of this imprint training she does?''

''I've heard about all I want to,'' he said, draining his glass. ''Where did you say the yearbooks were?''

His mother pointed him toward the den. He soon found Tally's senior picture. The thin face, the large, long-lashed eyes and full lips were only a pale hint of the beauty she would become. *Could* become. If she ever wore anything but those old jeans and baggy shirt and scuffed boots.

What in the hell was wrong with him? Looking her

up in the yearbook. What did it matter who she was and what she looked like fifteen years ago. All that mattered was that he needed her to get the ranch in shape. He closed the yearbook with a loud snap and told himself to get off his duff. Instead, like an idiot, he sat down in his father's leather armchair and opened the book again. And stared at her picture once more, his forehead creased in a frown.

The years faded away. Prom night. The dance he didn't go to. The bar he went to instead. The countless beers. The party at the beach. The bonfire and wishing on a star and a promise. A promise? What was that all about?

He got to his feet. The yearbook fell to the floor still opened to her picture. Oh, yes. It all came back to him now. Oh, Lord. He'd been so drunk that night he'd promised to marry Tally James. Fortunately they all knew he wasn't sober at the time. No one, not even Tally expected him to keep that promise. Did they?

# Chapter Two

That night he had dinner at the country club with his mother. He made polite conversation while his mind remained in turmoil. The next day, after a sleepless night, he dialed Tally's number, and after an eternity she answered.

"Where were you?" he asked sharply.

"In the barn. I'm still there. What do you want?"

"Do you know who this is?"

"Yes, I know who this is."

"I saw good old Dwight last night. Thanks to your description, I recognized him right away."

"Where was that?" she asked.

"Is that important?" He hated to say "the country club." It was one of the reasons he left Harmony. The same old families at the same old club. His parents' friends, not his. People from the right side of the tracks only. The assumption that he'd take his father's place on the board of directors still lingering. The country club was a place for the "haves," but not the "have-nots."

He had a feeling Tally James, as a have-not, might not want to hear about the country club.

"I just wondered. What did he say?"

"He said it was good to see me."

"That must have made your day."

"Considering the reception I've gotten elsewhere, yes."

She drew in a sharp breath as she caught his meaning.

"What did you expect?"

"I don't know. A cold drink would have been nice."

"After criticizing the way I run your ranch?"

"After helping you fix your fence."

"*Your* fence. I don't have time for cold drinks. If I did, I'd have one right now. But I've got a class of beginners waiting for me, so if you don't mind..."

"Dwight said he could see us at ten on Monday morning," Jed said.

"Why bother? Why didn't he just hand over the money on the spot?"

"At the country club?" he asked. "That's not the way it's done."

"Well, pardon me. I wouldn't know. I've never been there," she said. Her voice shook so slightly he almost missed it, and he kicked himself for coming off like the rich snob she took him for.

"I didn't mean that."

"What did you mean?" she asked.

"I want you to come with me on Monday morning. I told him you would. He'll have questions I can't answer. About the income and expenses. Profit and loss. Bring your books. You said you had plans. Estimates. Dwight wants to see them. So do I. Bring whatever you've got."

"All right. Okay. I have to go now."

He hung up, vastly relieved she hadn't brought up that

ridiculous offer he'd made while under the influence, but
worried that she eventually would, which would embarrass them both. But he was looking forward to Monday.
It had nothing to do with seeing Tally again. It had everything to do with getting on with the project, starting
with the bank loan. The sooner he got the loan, the
sooner he could fix up the ranch and put it on the market.
The better job they did, the more money it would bring
in and the quicker he could get on with his plans for the
future.

And Tally? She was a novelty. At the same time she
was part of his past. A very small part, considering the
role she was playing now. He didn't know what to expect from her. Didn't know what she expected from him.
Though it should be obvious. The answers were "nothing" and "nothing."

Unaccustomed as she was to meetings with the bank
president in his office, Tally was uncertain about how to
dress. So she wore a totally feminine flowered dress and
carried a totally businesslike briefcase under her arm.
She quickened her step when she saw Jed pacing back
and forth in front of the bank on Main Street. He was
looking at his watch.

When she got close enough, he grabbed her by the
wrists so forcefully she dropped her briefcase. Releasing
her, he picked it up and handed it to her.

"I was afraid you weren't coming," he explained.

She tightened her grip on her briefcase, breathing as
hard as if she'd run all the way there. "I said I would."

"Do you always do what you say?"

"Don't you?"

"No."

At least he was honest. And she had no wish to remind

him of what he'd promised fifteen years ago. He would just laugh. It was a joke, after all. Why would she want to marry someone who thought he was too good for her, the town and everyone in it?

Dwight was cordial. Dwight was downright jovial, making small talk and dredging up memories of the senior prank, drag races down Main Street and the marching band. When he asked Jed what he'd been up to, Jed gave a rundown of the various businesses he'd been in, all so impressive it made Tally realize all over again how different they were. While he'd been running an airline, Tally had been pulling a horse trailer around the county, showing other people's horses, and teaching other people to ride. Finally Dwight got down to business.

"So, Jed, what's this about a loan? Not thinking of coming back to settle in Harmony, are we?"

"No. In fact, I'm planning on selling the ranch. But first I'd like to make some improvements."

"How much do you want to borrow?"

Jed looked at Tally. At the dress that clung to those delectable curves he'd only imagined the other day. At the swell of her breasts and the shape of her hips. He got a glimpse of her long legs. Once long and skinny. Now long and shapely. And he wanted to see more. He felt like he was suffocating in that small office.

When Tally pulled some papers from her briefcase, he finally dragged his eyes away from her body and looked at the figures. They blurred. What was wrong with him, the crackerjack businessman, unable to concentrate on business?

He looked at the figures again, carefully. And saw that Tally was using a spreadsheet to chart the finances. She'd figured how much he would need to invest in order to resell the ranch for two and a half million and how long it would take. What else did he expect from the girl who excelled at math?

When she mentioned the amount, Dwight frowned. "That's a lot of money," he said.

"Of course it's a lot of money," Jed said, "but the ranch is worth a lot. Or it will be when we're finished."

"We?"

"Tally here is my tenant, as you know. She's agreed to act as my foreman for the remodeling." He stole a glance at her. Unable to remember if she'd really agreed or not. Her face was calm. She was poised and graceful, as if she went to see the bank president every day. If he were on the other side of the desk, he'd fork over the money so fast it would make her head spin. He had an irrational desire to try to make Tally James's level head spin.

So why was Dwight hesitating? Besides Jed's being a friend, and a known quantity, it made good business sense to lend him the money. Jed drummed his fingers on one denim-clad knee. "What's the problem, Dwight?"

"Here's the deal, Jed. Our loans are earmarked for family farms or ranches. It's a way we have of encouraging families to stay on the land instead of selling out to developers, and it helps the young people who want to stay in Harmony and raise a family. You say you want to borrow money to improve the place in order to sell. How do we know you're going to sell to a family? If you're asking two and a half million, what kind of family could afford that kind of money?"

Jed leaned forward in the vinyl chair. "You never know, Dwight."

"That's the point. We wouldn't know. But we'd be pretty sure you'd have to sell to a developer to get that kind of return on your investment, or the bank's investment. Now, if you were a married man, planning to settle on your ranch, where your daddy raised you, and his daddy before him, I'd have no problem lending you what you're asking for.'' He paused and tilted his head to one side. ''But you're not, are you?''

''What, married? No, but what…''

''Got any plans?'' the banker asked.

''To get married? No.'' As if it was any of his business. He reminded himself that this was why he'd left Harmony in the first place. To escape this kind of small-town mentality. The pressure to settle down and get married, to do what everyone else did.

Jed thought briefly of the women he might have married, of the women he could have married. For a brief moment he wished he'd married one of them. He'd have the money in his pocket by now. But which woman from his past would have agreed to live on a ranch in the middle of nowhere?

''You can't do this, Dwight. It's not legal.''

''It's not only legal, it's morally right. You've got to admit that, don't you, Jed?''

''No, I don't.''

''Family values being what they are.''

Jed stared into Dwight's beady brown eyes and fought off the urge to deck him. Who was he to tell Jed he couldn't borrow money from the bank because he didn't live his life according to Harmony standards, where home and hearth came first?

He clenched his hands into fists, feeling the adrenaline pump through his body. Just as he was about to give Dwight a piece of his mind or a punch in the nose, Tally stuffed the papers back in her briefcase and stood up. Dwight stood and shook hands with Tally, then with Jed.

"See you both," he beamed, looking from one to the other, "at the reunion. Should be quite a wing-ding."

"So I hear," Jed muttered.

Dwight opened the door to his office and they filed out.

Jed stood on the sidewalk outside the bank and rocked back on the heels of his new boots. "Did he say what I think he said?" he asked Tally. "That I have to get married to get a loan?"

She nodded.

"I can't believe it. It's times like this I wish I hadn't stopped drinking."

"Have you?"

"Yes, I have. At least before noon. Or before I fly. Are you opposed to drinking?" he asked.

"Not at all," she said coolly. "I often get up and have a shot of whiskey before breakfast just to get going." She'd show him she was just as sophisticated as he was.

He grinned. "And I thought you were some kind of goody-goody."

"And I thought you were some kind of hotshot businessman."

"So did I. I feel like I've been hit over the head with a baseball bat. And I never saw it coming. That's the hell of it. I thought I had it. I thought I'd walk out of there with the cash. Piece of cake."

"I did, too."

"Well, I sure as hell don't want to drink alone. So I'm not going to drink at all. What about tonight? Are you free to do some serious commiserating?"

"I'm not sure I'm in the mood. After all, if you don't get the loan, you can't fix up the ranch, and if you can't fix it up then you can't sell it and I can stay where I am." She couldn't help a small, triumphant smile.

"Your logic is almost as good as your math. But not quite. It's based on a faulty premise. Because I *will* get the loan."

Tally shifted from one leather thong sandal to the other. She had to get away from this man. He disturbed her, he tempted her, he irritated her. He was taking this rejection surprisingly well. She reminded herself that he wasn't in danger of starving. He was still rich. Maybe he was only rich on paper, but he was still rich. Whereas she was poor. On paper and otherwise. And if he sold the ranch *she* might be in danger of starving.

She told herself these things because Jed had never looked so appealing. So vulnerable. So disarming. So dangerous. So determined. She took a deep breath and tried to stop the memories from flooding back of Jed as a wild teenager, sitting behind her in math class, sullen and angry. Of the few occasions when his path had crossed hers. The last being the beach party.

If only she could forget as easily as he had. But he had packed his life with adventure, soaring among the clouds in small planes. While she'd been here in Harmony, earthbound, doing what she did best, what she loved. And now he wanted her to commiserate with him. Of all the nerve! If it was up to her he'd go back where he came from, and she'd continue to send him rent checks. It was hard to believe she'd be better off when the ranch sold. How could he possibly pay her enough to buy a ranch of her own? And how could any other ranch ever compare to White Horse?

"I don't think so," she said. "I'm busy tonight."

"This isn't my day. First I get hit over the head by a banker, then I strike out with you. See you later."

She raised her eyebrows. "Are you leaving? Giving up?"

"Give up? After some small-town banker turns me down for a loan? Not a chance. You wouldn't give up, would you?"

"Depends on how badly I wanted the money. You haven't told me what you're going to do with it."

"I'm going to buy out my partner and get control of the airline we own."

She rocked back on her heels in surprise. "You never told me you owned an airline. Which one is it? TWA, United?"

He smiled ruefully. "A little commuter airline you've probably never heard of. But one that people in some remote areas depend on for freight and passenger service."

"So when it's all yours, what will you do with it?" she asked.

"Go after the mail service, expand into remote areas. Do some med-evac work. Lease prop planes that are cheaper to operate. That's my plan."

Tally stood on the sidewalk staring at him. He seemed so serious, so focused, so different from the shallow playboy she'd always thought he was. She had more questions on the tip of her tongue about what routes he was talking about and if he flew the planes himself and where the headquarters were, but she didn't have time to stand in front of the bank talking with the sexiest, liveliest, most interesting and richest man in town.

And she really shouldn't find out any more about his life outside of Harmony, because the more she knew the more intrigued she became. And since she was not in the business of getting her heart broken, and she knew that would happen when he left, she smiled a brief smile that was gone before it started and said, "Gotta go."

He grabbed her arm and spun her around. "Not so fast."

The fog that hovered over Jed's mind lifted. His vision was suddenly brilliantly clear in the bright sunlight. The solution to the problem was right in front of him. He felt like laughing out loud. He felt like lifting Tally into the air and spinning her around.

"I've got it," he said, smashing his fist into his other hand with a loud smack. "It's so obvious. So simple. I'll marry *you!*"

# Chapter Three

"Win some, lose some," Jed muttered to himself as he drove home. But these days all he did was lose—the value of the ranch, then the loan and now this. Damn Tally's stubborn hide. "Thanks, but no thanks," she'd said. That was all.

While he stood there with his mouth hanging open, she'd turned on her heel and left him standing on the sidewalk watching her sashay down the street, head held high, hips swaying just enough to drive an ordinary man crazy. But he was not an ordinary man. And he was not accustomed to being turned down.

Nobody said no to Jed Whitmore. Not without an explanation. And nobody reneged on a bargain, no matter how long ago it was made or under what conditions. He hadn't wanted to bring it up, but she was leaving him no choice. He was going to hold her to their bargain. She hadn't seen the last of him. Not by a long shot. He glared at his own image in his rearview mirror.

* * *

Jed Whitmore thought it wasn't his day because he'd been hit with bad news from his banker, but Tally was kicked by a nervous horse, knocked down by a swinging barn door and chewed out royally by the angry parent of a student. At six o'clock she hobbled back to the house, left her knee-high rubber boots at the door and grabbed the wall phone in the kitchen to stop the insistent ringing.

"Tally, it's me, Suzy. Angela saw you and Jed Whitmore at the bank this morning. What's going on?"

Tally fought off a stab of disappointment when she heard Suzy's voice. Not that she thought it would be Jed. She'd turned him down, after all. On the other hand, he didn't seem like the type to take no from her any more than he would take no from a banker.

Tally pulled up a stool and rested her elbows on the breakfast bar. "Nothing's going on. He just wanted the accounts from the ranch. So I gave them to him."

"At the bank?"

"Yes at the bank. Where should I have done it, at the Tastee-Freez?"

"I'd let Jed Whitmore buy me a Tastee-Freez any day of the week." Suzy giggled. "Unless he can't afford it. I heard he was at the bank to borrow money."

"I wouldn't know," Tally said, unwilling to confirm Jed's worst impression of Harmony as a place for small-town gossip. "Why don't you give him a call? Maybe you can buy *him* a Tastee-Freez," Tally suggested.

"He's not home. Martha's father was at the Red Pump and he saw Jed at the bar."

"Same old Jed," Tally murmured.

"No," Suzy said. "Not the same. He was drinking a cup of coffee. Yes, coffee. Sounds like he's changed. But then I haven't seen him for years, not since high school. Not since prom night, actually. The night he promised he'd—''

"Look Suzy, my head hurts, I've got a gash in my shin, blood running down my ankle and a pounding headache.''

"How does he look?'' Suzy asked, undeterred by Tally's list of injuries.

Tally took a deep breath then let it out slowly, picturing his muscles flexing as he nailed new slats to the fence, picturing his wide grin when he asked her to marry him and the shock on his face when she turned him down. "Fine. He looks just fine.''

"Better or worse than he used to?'' Suzy asked.

"I don't remember what he used to look like,'' she lied. "My mind is a blank. Did I mention the lump on my head?''

"Maybe you've got amnesia. Because I remember *exactly* how he looked, with that little scar over his eyebrow from his motorcycle accident. And the blue eyes. Have you ever seen eyes that color before...or since?'' Suzy said dreamily. "Say hi to him for me when you see him again. If you remember.''

Tally hung up and limped into her bedroom to take a shower. As the hot water beat mercifully against her skin, she wondered who else remembered what he'd said. Suzy did, she did...did Jed?

Who was Jed Whitmore, anyway? Did anyone in town really know? Was he still the town rebel, obsessed with getting richer and more successful than his father? Or had he come to grips with his heritage and mellowed with the years. She had to admit he'd been fair with her. So far. After all, he could hire someone else. Marry someone else. Then wait till her lease was up and turn her out in the street. Instead he offered her the job and a chance to save some money to buy what she wanted most. Rebel or nice guy? Tally suspected the truth was somewhere in between. And so it went with the saga of the Whitmore family, providing the rest of the town with enough gossip to last several lifetimes.

After Tally showered and plastered her shin with Band-Aids, she took two aspirin and went to the kitchen in the caretaker's house where she'd lived ever since she'd first rented the place. She was staring at the meager contents of her refrigerator when Jed Whitmore knocked on the back door.

Her face flamed. Her heart pounded. She wasn't dressed for company, nor was she in the mood to socialize with the man whose proposal she'd turned down earlier that day.

"I thought you were at the Red Pump tonight," she said, wishing she'd at least worn a bra under her oversize T-shirt. Pretending she didn't notice the flat cardboard box in his hand or the six-pack of soda under his arm. The smell of cheese and sausage wafted into the kitchen.

He brushed past her, set the pizza on the table and the six-pack on the counter. "I was, but I got hungry and I don't like to eat alone. Do you?"

"Yes, I mean no, but I don't recall..."

"I don't recall your inviting me to dinner, either, but you must have, since I'm not the type to barge in unannounced. I thought I'd bring the food and drink, just in case...." He put his hands on her shoulders, shoved her down into a kitchen chair.

Numbly she sat and stared at the pizza as if she hadn't eaten for days, when it had only been since her breakfast of one slice of toast. Once he had set two glasses of cola on the table and sat down across from her, she starting eating, thinking she'd never tasted anything so delicious.

He ate two large pieces, while he looked around at the flowered curtains she'd hung at the windows, at the copper pots she'd hung from the ceiling, without giving a hint as to whether he'd ever ventured into the servants' quarters before. Finally he leaned back in his chair and looked at her with those amazing electric blue eyes.

"You're quiet tonight," he remarked.

"I don't know what to say, except thank you and I'm sorry."

He nodded. "Sorry you turned me down. Good. I knew you'd come to your senses."

She shook her head. "Sorry about letting the place go downhill. I should have tried harder to get in touch with you."

She wanted to tell him she'd been so worried about her mother she just couldn't worry about the ranch declining. But that would mean she'd have to tell the whole sorry story from the beginning. Including her father's business failure and subsequent suicide. Maybe everyone knew about it, but maybe they didn't. Maybe Jed didn't. Maybe he didn't know how he'd died.

She wanted her father to be remembered as a man who loved the town, who'd served the people in it and given his best until the end. She wanted her mother to be remembered as a wife who'd stood by her husband, the best she could as his business failed and he went bankrupt.

But how could she discuss such financial problems with a man who'd been born with a silver spoon in his mouth? He might think he needed money, but he had no idea what it was like to receive a Christmas basket from the church or owe everyone in town from the grocer to the power company.

He observed her carefully. "Since we're apologizing," he said at last, "I'm sorry for dropping in on you unannounced."

She wished he wouldn't turn polite on her. Because she knew why he was there. She knew why he'd brought her dinner and plied her with cold drinks from the convenience store. He wanted something. He wanted her to marry him, and she wasn't going to do it.

If she ever got married, it would be for love and not money. She had to keep that in mind because the combined effects of her injuries, the aspirin and the hot food were making her feel like a spineless jellyfish who'd do anything he asked. She had to hope and pray he wouldn't ask again. Not tonight. Tomorrow she could say no. Tonight all she could do was wish she'd worn something more protective, like a suit of armor, instead of a T-shirt that advertised the local rodeo.

"That's all right," she said. But it wasn't all right at all. He couldn't come barging onto her ranch or his ranch, without warning. Without giving her time to shore up her defenses against the best-looking man to ever leave Harmony. Or stay in Harmony. She was too vulnerable to a man who looked at her the way he was looking, with concern in his gaze. When concern turned to something else, something that turned his eyes a shade darker, her pulse quickened.

She struggled to change the subject, to find a subject, any subject. "Still feeling bad about the loan?" she asked. And instantly wished she hadn't. The subject of the loan would lead to the subject of the marriage.

"Don't worry, we'll get the loan." He covered her hand with his and lightly caressed her palm with the pad of his thumb. A gesture that was meant to be reassuring, no doubt, but coming from him bordered on the erotic. Her head spun, her mouth went dry. The way he said *we* caused panic to rise in her throat. He was going to start on the marriage thing again. Just when she wasn't thinking clearly.

She wanted to say, "How? How will you get the loan?" But the words lodged in her throat and she couldn't speak.

He leaned forward and ran his broad fingers over the bump on her forehead. "How'd you get that?"

Her heart thumped so loudly it drowned out the chimes of the grandfather clock in the living room. She licked her dry lips and took a sip of cola. "I...uh...I got in the way of a swinging barn door. That's nothing. You should see my leg."

"I'd like to," he said with a lazy grin.

She sucked in a sharp breath and pulled her hand away. He was teasing her, flirting with her. Why not, there wasn't much else to do in Harmony. But she wasn't used to it. Didn't know how to handle being somebody's temporary diversion.

She stood and winced as she put weight on her injured leg. "I'll make some coffee."

He got to his feet. "Sit down. I'll do it." He took the pot out of her hand. She sat down and watched him measure the grains into a filter. "You're surprised I can do anything but collect rent checks, aren't you?" he asked. "Just like everyone else in this town, you thought I was a spoiled brat."

"You seemed to have everything you wanted," she said, watching him move around the kitchen as if he was completely at home. "The car, the college education, travel..."

"Expectations, pressure to be somebody I wasn't," he added. "My dad had big plans for me from the day I was born. He had my life all mapped out."

"Yes, you mentioned something about it that night...a long time ago." Oh, damn, she'd brought up the prom night beach party.

"Did I?" He glanced in her direction. A glance that told her he remembered and that he knew she remembered, too. "I was bitter about it. No wonder I didn't have any friends and I had to latch on to yours."

"Those weren't my friends around the fire. Except for Suzy. Anyway, about your father..."

"He taught me a lot about money."

"I hear it makes the world go round," she said.

"But it's the root of all evil," he added.

"Are you saying you could get along without it?" she asked, propping her leg on his vacant chair to take the pressure off.

"I did get along without it," he said as the coffee dripped through the filter into the pot. "All the money I have now I made on my own. My dad left everything to my mother. Except for the ranch. I was on my own. At the time I was angry. Now I realize it was the best thing for me."

When it was ready, Jed poured coffee into two cups and set them on the table. Before she could move, he lifted her leg off the chair with one hand under her ankle, sat down and put her smooth, bare leg across his knees. He casually stirred his coffee with one hand and just as casually laid the other on her knee as if he'd done it a hundred times, when he'd never touched her at all—although he'd thought about it.

"You don't want to like me, do you?" he asked, stroking the soft, sensitive inside of her knee.

He watched her silver-gray eyes darken to the color of the evening sky. She could have pulled her leg away, she could have told him to stop, but she didn't. Her lips parted, but no sound came out. He stared shamelessly as her nipples puckered and pressed against her cotton T-shirt. He felt a tightening in his groin as his body responded.

"Jed, I do like you, but..."

"But the answer is still no. Don't worry about it. I'll find somebody else to marry."

With that she jerked her leg away and braced her hands against the table.

He stood and sauntered to the door. He'd come on too fast. He, Mr. Cool, who never let a woman know he was interested. He hadn't meant to come on to her at all. Now he'd scared her away. *Such a lovely girl and after all she's been through.* Her father killing himself. Her mother unable to take care of herself. And he thought he'd had it bad living up to his father's expectations.

There was something about her. Something besides her energy and high spirits and her natural elegance that called to something deep inside him. He felt sorry for her, of course. So did everyone else in town. But he felt something else—call it admiration. And she stirred feelings in him he'd long forgotten. For her or for Harmony or for his wasted youth?

He said good-night before he closed the door behind him. At least he thought he said it. All he really remembered was Tally standing in the kitchen, hands on her slim hips, her curly hair still damp from the shower, the smell of coffee in the air. And a look in her eyes that haunted him for days to come. The look that said yes while her lips said no.

Tally didn't see Jed during the next week, for which she was profoundly grateful. She couldn't afford to have a millionaire playboy upset her equilibrium by plying her with pizza and the promise of a marriage of convenience. He was out of her league. She knew it and he knew it. That's why she hadn't heard from him or seen him. He'd found someone else. Someone more suitable. But who?

Tally knew that if she wanted to hear any news about anyone, she should ask Suzy. But she couldn't just call and ask her. Her best friend would jump to the wrong conclusions. Tally had to run into her by accident. Which she did a few days later at the feed and fuel on Main Street where Suzy used to work. Tally was buying oats and Suzy was perusing the bulletin board at the front of the store.

When she saw Tally, Suzy beckoned to her and pointed to a picture on the bulletin board which advertised everything from livestock to motor homes. "Looks like Marv Garnett's selling one of his mares," she said.

Tally squinted at the color photo of the horse. Instantly she recognized the sleek lines of the mare she'd seen at Plentywood Farm and her distinctive pale color. "She's so beautiful," Tally said with a sigh. "Do you know how much he wants for her?"

"More than you can afford."

Tally blew a strand of hair off her forehead. "I'm sick of people telling me what I can't afford. How much does he want?"

"Ten thousand dollars. That's what I heard."

"Thank you." Grimly Tally lifted three sacks of grain and a stall mat to the counter with a loud thump and looked around impatiently for the clerk.

"He's gone," Suzy said. "Left town."

"Who left?" Tally asked. "Marv or the clerk?"

"Don't play innocent with me, Ms. James," Suzy said in a stage whisper. "You know who I'm talking about.

I happen to know why the man couldn't get a loan at the bank. I know that you know, too."

"Could you be talking about Jed Whitmore?" Tally asked, looking over her shoulder nervously. "Let me put it another way. Could you be talking about anyone else?"

"Who else in our class has only gotten better looking with the years, besides you of course. Who else was in *People Weekly* last year with some socialite he was supposed to be engaged to? Who else has enough money to buy and sell the whole town?"

"Then why does he want a loan from the bank?" Tally asked.

"To buy out his partner in the airline."

"Well, that's not surprising," Tally said, trying not to act surprised that Suzy knew. "That's just what I would do, wouldn't you?"

"Do you know how much it costs to buy half an airline?" Suzy demanded.

"I don't even know how much it costs to buy three sacks of oats and a stall mat," Tally said, wishing the missing clerk would show up so she could pay her bill and get out of there.

"Can you believe he's really coming to the reunion?" Suzy asked. "After he gets back from wherever he's gone to."

"Are you sure about that?"

"He sent in his reservation."

"His *mother* sent in his reservation."

"Who told you that?"

"He did."

"You're holding out on me," Suzy said. "What else did he tell you?"

"He told me he waited two hours for you at the

Tastee-Freez. But you didn't show. He thinks you're a tease and a troublemaker. And he wants you to call him the minute you get the braces off your teeth."

Suzy gave a hoot of laughter, displaying a mouthful of perfectly straight teeth. Then she picked up a double weave shantung hat from a rack and jammed it on Tally's head, covering her ears. "I don't believe a word you've said. I've spilled my soul to you and you've never confided one damn thing to me."

"That's because I have nothing to confide," Tally said.

"That's because you don't trust me. You think I'll blab it all over town."

"You? Blab?" Tally said removing the hat from her head. "I swear, if I have anything to say, you'll be the first to hear it. Oh, good, here she is. Now maybe I can get out of here."

Suzy watched silently while the owner's daughter totaled the figures. Then Suzy helped Tally carry the oats to her truck.

"Does it strike you odd that you and I and Jed are the only people from our class who aren't married and never have been? What's wrong with us?" Suzy asked plaintively as she stacked a sack of oats in the back of her friend's truck. "I mean, I haven't worn braces since I was sixteen, but nobody around here notices."

"The ones that notice don't meet your high standards. I don't know about Jed, but I know that you are too picky for your own good. What are you waiting for, Prince Charming?" Tally asked.

"Is there something wrong with that?" Suzy asked.

"No, of course not," Tally said, getting into her truck. She leaned out the window. "Princes often show up in

Harmony, looking for someone who fits the glass slipper. The thing is, they usually come disguised as frogs.''

"Ugh," Suzy said. "Then how are we supposed to know who they really are? No, don't tell me, you have to kiss them first."

Tally nodded ruefully and pulled out of the parking lot. Instead of worrying about Prince Charming, she worried about the reunion. She dreaded it. She looked forward to it. She was scared to go. She was more scared not to. Exactly the way she'd felt fifteen years ago. She thought she'd matured and had her priorities straight. But here she was just as worried about a silly party as she'd been when she was a teenager. The funny thing was, she hadn't given it a thought, hadn't even worried about what to wear to it, until Jed came back.

That same day she found herself at the drygoods store buying a bolt of pale silk and a pattern for a designer dress. Which meant she'd have to spend the next few evenings cutting and sewing instead of reading about equine diseases. And why? To impress a bunch of people she'd known all her life. It made no sense at all. And Tally had always been sensible. Until now.

Everyone said the committee had done a great job. The high school gym was decorated with blue and yellow crepe paper streamers just like it was fifteen years ago. They'd duplicated the refreshments and the music. Potato chips and dried-out sandwiches and watery punch.

Shrieks of recognition and sighs of disbelief filled the drafty gym. There were hugs and kisses and even a few tears, as the classmates stuck name tags to their lapels and filed in. Many Harmony High graduates had stayed right there in Harmony, worked for their fathers and married their high school sweethearts, but others moved to Las Vegas, Portland or Spokane and were back for the party.

Tally, with butterflies in the pit of her stomach, feeling self-conscious in her new dress that she'd just finished hemming that afternoon, stood in front of a large easel looking at faded photographs taken during their senior year. A deep voice interrupted her reverie.

"Recognize anyone?" he asked. His breath was warm on the back of her neck. A shiver of awareness ran up her spine and then down again.

She didn't turn around. She didn't need to. She knew who it was. She pointed to a boy in a football uniform. "Here's our friend Dwight, twenty pounds lighter."

"Twenty?"

"All right, fifty. There's Suzy, my best friend, in her cheerleader outfit."

"Isn't that Josh Gentry with Molly? No need to ask what happened to them, they had happily ever after written all over them." A trace of unexpected envy crept into his voice.

Tally bit her lip. "Molly died two years ago."

"Oh, God, I'm sorry. I didn't know."

Tally blinked back a tear and pointed to another picture. "Here's the self-made millionaire."

"Looking like a self-made jerk. And feeling like one, too. I haven't changed, have I?"

She stole a glance at him out of the corner of her eye. And gasped. He was wearing a dark suit that fit as if it had been made for him. It probably had. A striped shirt and a patterned tie and wingtip shoes. He was gorgeous. He was big-time, big city and head and shoulders above everyone else in Harmony. Had he changed? The answer was yes and no. Despite his wealth and good looks and success, there was still a streak of insecurity under that smooth exterior. And he was just as out of place as ever. But there was something else, something new that hadn't been there before. She just didn't know what it was.

Tally turned back to the pictures. "Where are you?" he asked, scanning the photographs.

Before she could answer, Jed felt someone pound him on the back. Someone hugged him, and someone else thrust a glass of punch into his hand. Out of the corner of his eye he saw Tally drift away as the scene turned into the one from his worst nightmare, and he cursed the day he'd agreed to attend this affair.

Hours went by. He shook hands with more men and he kissed more women than he had in the past year. He danced and he smiled until his face hurt, and he drank about a gallon of that god-awful punch. By twelve o'clock he had a raging headache. The music blared from the overhead speaker—a song he hadn't heard for fifteen years.

Time spun backward. He was eighteen and too good for Harmony. Too sophisticated for a high school prom. Instead of going, he got drunk at the bar outside of town, then rode in on his motorcycle in time for the last dance. A song billowed from the front door of the gym.

It all came back, one piece at a time. The night, the dance, the song. And Tally. The funny little scarecrow who climbed into the back seat of Josh's car for a ride to the beach. Where the hell was she now?

With his arm braced against the wall, he squinted through the haze of cigarette smoke looking for her. Instead he saw her friend Suzy.

"You seen Tally?" he asked.

Suzy nodded. "She's out front." She took him by the arm and walked him through the gym, stepping over smashed potato chips and crushed paper cups on their way out the front door. Tally was sitting on the steps, her chin on her knees, staring across dark fields in the pale moonlight. Hearing their footsteps, she turned and looked at them.

"Here he is," Suzy announced. "The man voted most likely to break hearts and speed records. Did you succeed, Jed?"

"With the speed records," he admitted, sitting down next to Tally on the top step, wishing his head would clear. Wishing he could start all over, if not his high school career, at least his return to Harmony.

"What about the hearts?" Suzy said, tapping her toe on the bottom step, looking up at them.

"Not many. But I've still got time. I'm not married yet," he said pointedly.

An empty cola can slipped out of Tally's hands and rolled down the steps. Jed chased it and handed it back to her. He brushed her hand with his. Deliberately. Their eyes met and held for a long, breathless moment. Then he sat back down on the step next to her, pressing his thigh tight against hers, feeling the heat from her body transfer to his.

Suzy kept talking. "I'm not married, either. And neither is Tally. Makes you wonder, doesn't it. What's wrong with us?"

"I know what's wrong with me. I'm sick." He frowned. "What did they put in that punch?"

"Sugar and water and some red stuff," Suzy said. "It's late and I'm leaving. Anyone want a ride?"

"No, thanks," Jed said with a restraining hand on Tally's arm.

Suzy's gaze fixed on Jed's hand on Tally's arm. "Oh. I see. Sure. Of course." She smiled knowingly and started walking backward down the walkway. "Call me tomorrow, Tally," she said. "You promised."

"You make a lot of promises," Jed said to Tally when Suzy was out of sight. "Do you remember the one you made after the prom?"

"At the lake? No."

"You said you'd marry me in fifteen years, if neither one of us was married."

"I couldn't have."

"But you did. And you don't remember. How do you think that makes me feel?"

"Relieved?" she asked.

He draped his arm loosely around her shoulder, and she stifled the urge to lean against him, and breathe in the heady scent of wealth and power and blatant sexual prowess.

"I'm hurt," he said.

"Just because I don't remember some stupid, silly juvenile agreement made in jest."

"Maybe you were jesting, but I wasn't."

"Oh, come on, Jed. I know what this is about. Hasn't anyone ever turned you down before?"

"I've never asked anyone to marry me before. What about you, how many men have you turned down? Plenty, I'd guess by the way you handled it. Just a 'thanks but no thanks' and walk away. Take no prisoners. Give no second chances. Yes, I admire your cool."

Tally shifted uneasily, tugging at the edge of her skirt.

"I would have let it go, you know. I would have respected your decision. If I hadn't remembered that you promised," he said, standing and pulling her up with him. He drew his eyebrows together until they almost met. "What is that damned perfume of yours, anyway?"

"Tea Rose."

He pulled her close and drank in the scent of her skin and her hair. It made him so dizzy he had to lean against her. She felt warm and soft and so sexy he felt his blood pressure rise to dangerous levels. She had to marry him. She promised, and she was going to keep her promise, dammit.

"So, what do you say?" he asked.

"I say we go back and get in my truck, and I'll drive you home."

"About getting married."

"Don't be ridiculous. You don't want to marry me," she said desperately. "I'm not your type."

"What is my type?" he asked.

"Some beautiful socialite. One who's got enough money to buy the other half of the airline for you."

He shook his head. "No such person. You're the one I want."

"Tomorrow you'll wake up and realize what a bad idea it is," she said.

"It was Dwight's idea."

"He suggested you get married. But not to me. He never mentioned my name."

"Of course not. But he was looking right at you."

"That's because I was sitting across from him. My marrying you doesn't make any sense."

"Oh yes it does. I need a wife to get a loan. You need money. You must need money. For something. What about the horse and the ranch you wished for?"

"Yes, of course, I still want those things, but..."

"But not enough to marry me. I understand that. But it'll be in name only. I won't force myself on you. And only until we get the place ready to sell." His mind was whirling. He had no idea if he was making any sense or not. He only knew he wouldn't take no for an answer. If they had to stand there all night.

"Let's talk about this tomorrow," she said.

"It *is* tomorrow."

"Let's talk about this when you're feeling better then."

"I'm feeling fine."

It was true. His head had stopped pounding as soon as he'd left the gym, and by the time they reached her truck parked behind the school, he was determined not to let her out of his sight until she'd said yes. He hadn't made his own fortune by taking no for an answer. From anybody. But then he'd seldom run into anybody quite like her.

From the first time he'd seen her he'd admired her gumption. He'd never forgotten the day he walked into her father's hardware store after school with his buddies to buy a wrench to adjust the spark plugs on his motorcycle. While he'd been making his selection, the other guys had leaned on the counter and asked her where the condoms were. Looking over the tool rack, he'd seen her blush furiously as they had teased her.

His supercool attitude had suddenly shattered. In a flash he'd shoved all three guys out the front door, leaving Tally staring at them, wide-eyed and speechless. Her chin held high, staring straight ahead. He'd left the wrench behind for another day. A day that never came. He bought all his tools from then on at the big chain hardware store that opened outside town and so did everyone else. Which was, he supposed, the beginning of the end for the mom and pop store.

"Think about it," he said returning abruptly to the present. "It makes sense. You know the ranch. You seem to understand the financials. You need money."

And you smell so damned good. "And I'm not really a useless, rich snob," he added.

"No? What are you?"

She had him there. What was he? A successful businessman. But he had a feeling she didn't care. It was time to quit talking and start acting.

They rounded the corner of the school and walked toward the parking lot. Tally unlocked the door to her truck, but before she could open the door, Jed braced his arms against the side of the truck and trapped her.

This couldn't be happening, she thought, afraid to meet his gaze, afraid of what she'd see in those dark dangerous eyes. Her wildest dreams were blending with reality. She couldn't push him away in her dreams any more than she could in real life. And she didn't want to.

He tilted her chin with his thumb and with a helpless sigh, she lifted her face to his. His eyes were clear and focused. Midnight blue, they regarded her with something like amused affection.

"Relax, Tally," he said, with a roguish smile. "There's nothing to be afraid of." He ran his hands down her arms, his practiced touch soothing and exciting her at the same time.

He leaned forward, giving her a chance to turn her head, to deny him access to her mouth, but she didn't. She couldn't. His mouth was so close she could feel his warm breath fan her lips.

Then he kissed her. A mere brush of his lips across hers, tempting, tantalizing, making her want more.

He gave her more. He gave her a whole series of kisses that sizzled and burned her lips. A dazzling array of kisses that left her breathless and giddy. She opened her lips and let his tongue dance with hers. She tasted fruit punch and inhaled the masculine scent of expensive leather and fine wool.

This never would have happened fifteen years ago. Never could have. Not to Natalie James, the girl whose date ran off with someone else. But it was happening now and nothing would stop it.

Nothing but voices in the parking lot. Car doors being opened and slammed shut. He pulled her close in the shadow of her truck, so close she could feel the strength of his arousal through her silk dress. All her coherent thoughts dissipated and dissolved. She was caught in a firestorm of throbbing sexual desire like nothing she'd experienced in her life.

Was that why she'd never married anyone else? Because she was waiting for Jed Whitmore to come back and marry her? If that was the reason, she was crazy out of her mind. Because Jed Whitmore, while admittedly the sexiest man alive, was only using her to get what he wanted. What about her? Would she marry to get what she wanted? She would never be able to afford a stud for her stable. But she had a feeling if she married Jed, she'd get one for her bedroom.

# Chapter Four

With a surge of energy, Tally placed her hands on Jed's shoulders, pushed him away from her and opened the door to the truck. Undaunted, he walked around to the passenger side and got in beside her.

"What are you doing?" she asked, glaring at him.

"Didn't you offer me a ride home?" he asked.

"That was Suzy."

"She's gone," he said.

"Where's your car?"

"At home. I walked."

She sighed. "All right, fine."

They drove a few blocks through the quiet streets without speaking. Tally felt awkward, but Jed seemed completely at ease. He was even whistling the last song they'd heard at the dance. That song that was forever etched in her memory. She pulled up in front of his mother's house, keeping the engine running, hoping, praying he'd get out without another incident. Her lips still stung from his kisses, her skin still tingled from his touch.

He reached over and turned off the key in the ignition. She sucked in a startled breath. The silence enveloped them, a heavy silence filled with unfinished business and unfulfilled promises.

"You could do worse, you know," he said, "than to marry me."

"How?" she asked.

He laughed, a deep rumbling sound that caught her off guard. It was a heady feeling, knowing she could make him laugh and even make him want her. If only for a moment. She told herself all he wanted from her was a few hot kisses and a marriage of convenience.

"How could you do worse?" he asked. "You could marry an ax murderer. Or the village idiot. Maybe you think I come close."

She glanced at him, stifling a reluctant smile. Why did he have to be so damned attractive, so mellow, with his tie loosened, the light from the street lamp illuminating the planes of his face, his stubborn chin and his broad forehead.

"I don't have to marry anybody," she said.

"Of course not. But why haven't you?"

"There's nobody to marry. Not even an ax murderer. This is Harmony. Every eligible male either got married out of high school or left town." She looked down at her watch. "And now I've really got to go."

"Come in with me. I'll make coffee."

"Are you crazy? It's late. What about your mother?"

"She doesn't wait up for me. I promise I won't mention marriage again. Not tonight."

Before she could protest, he'd jumped out of the truck and come around to her side to open the door for her.

"Jed, no."

He pressed his index finger against her lips. "Shhh. You'll wake the neighbors." With his hands under her elbows he pried her out of her seat and pulled her on to the sidewalk. The next thing she knew she'd entered the house from the back door and was sitting on a ladder-backed chair at a glass-topped table, in a kitchen straight out of *Architecture Digest*. She was surrounded by pale oak cabinets, granite counters and a quarry tile floor, with the smell of freshly brewed coffee filling the air.

"Does anyone actually cook here?" she asked in a hushed whisper.

"Not that I know of." He set two cups of coffee on the table and sat across from her. Instead of drinking his coffee, he studied her with that penetrating gaze of his. The one that made her distinctly uneasy. Made her hands shake and her heart pound.

"This could get to be a habit," he remarked.

She shook her head. "I don't think so. I don't even like coffee."

"What about me?"

"You?" She picked up a spoon and stirred her coffee briskly, needlessly. "Of course I like you. But I'm not going to marry you. What would your mother say?"

"About what?" his mother said from the doorway.

Tally's spoon slipped from her grasp and clattered against the glass tabletop. Mrs. Whitmore was wearing a tailored plaid bathrobe with velvet lapels. Her silvery gray hair was swept back from her unlined face, and she looked like she'd just come from a week at a spa. She probably had.

"Hello, Tally," Jed's mother said graciously. "How are you, dear?"

"Fine, thank you."

"Did we wake you?" Jed asked.

"I smelled the coffee. What would I say about what?"

"About my marrying Tally."

Tally gripped the edge of her chair so she wouldn't fall off it. Through a haze she watched the expression on Jed's mother's aristocratic features. If she was shocked or revolted, she didn't show it. Perhaps nothing would shock or revolt her. She was that composed. Instead a smile played on her lips. "I'd say congratulations." She paused, turning her bright blue gaze so like her son's from Jed to Tally and back to Jed. "Should I?"

"That depends on Tally," Jed said as smoothly as if they were discussing adding a brood mare to the stables. "I'm having a hard time convincing her to marry me. It must be something I said. Or didn't say."

Tally's face flamed. She cleared her throat. "It's just...I mean..."

"She doesn't think she'll fit in."

"Fit in? One of the best riders in the whole county? Someone you've known most of your life? Of course she'll fit in," Mrs. Whitmore said. "So this is why you couldn't wait to look her up in your yearbook when you..."

"That's right," Jed interrupted.

If Tally hadn't known better she'd have thought Jed was embarrassed. But that couldn't be. Not smooth, suave, man-about-town Jed Whitmore. And yet he was staring into his coffee cup as if there might be something at the bottom. So he'd looked her up in the yearbook. She didn't have to look him up. She remembered exactly how he looked in those days. Tall and broad-shouldered even then, with his blond hair bleached by the summer sun.

The first time she'd seen him up close was one day during the summer after her freshman year in high school. It was at the Parker Ranch, where she was shoveling manure in exchange for riding privileges. She'd come around the corner of the barn pushing a wheelbarrow and crashed into him and Bo Parker, spattering both of them with brown stains all over their supercool shirts and dress pants.

"Whoa," Bo yelled, looking at her from over his sunglasses. "Watch where you're going."

"Sorry." What else could she say? What else could she do but turn bright red with shame?

"You better pick that stuff up," Bo ordered with a disdainful sniff.

"Wait a minute," Jed said. "It wasn't her fault. We crashed into her."

"It doesn't matter. She works here. C'mon, Jed."

But Jed stayed and helped her shovel the manure back into the wheelbarrow while Bo watched from a distance. Jed didn't say anything, he just worked alongside her quietly and efficiently, like the way he did the fence repair the other day. And then he was gone. Leaving her so shocked she forgot to thank him.

"Tally, what can I say?" his mother asked. "Jed has his flaws, heaven knows. He's a procrastinator, late for appointments and he always—"

"Isn't it past your bedtime?" Jed asked pointedly, getting to his feet. "I'm afraid we're keeping you up."

"I don't want to miss anything," his mother said. "But you're right. It is late. For me, that is. You young people can stay up as late as you want. I won't hear a thing." With that assurance she slipped out of the kitchen as suddenly as she'd arrived.

"Now what do you think?" Jed asked, noting Tally's

discomfort with an amused smile. Trust his mother to come up with something to embarrass them both.

"I think I ought to go home." Tally's face was flushed, her eyes on the framed family pictures on the wall.

"Don't go." Jed reached for her hand and held it tight. It was just possible she was wavering. And if so he didn't want her to leave before she'd committed herself. He knew instinctively that once she'd given her word, she wouldn't back down. He also knew that if he let her go tonight, she might never say yes in the cold light of day.

She bit her lip, but she didn't try to pull away. Her hand was warm and small in his. He rubbed his thumb over the calluses on her palm and felt a jolt of desire hit him when he least expected it. Desire and admiration. When she finally met his gaze he saw a matching flame of desire that made hope surge in his heart.

"Why is this so important to you?" she asked breathlessly.

"You know why. The loan, the airline, the future."

"That's all?"

He hesitated. This was not the time to scare her with talk of lust or whatever it was that flared between them. "This is not just important for me. It's going to mean a lot to you, too. I plan to pay you a large salary. Enough to make a down payment on your own place."

Her eyes widened. "Really?"

"Really. So is that a yes?" he asked.

"I guess so," she said in a small voice.

"Don't get carried away with enthusiasm," he said sarcastically.

"Yes. Yes. Okay." She jerked her hand away and stood up. "Now can I go home?"

He opened the back door for her and followed her to her truck. Relief flooded his whole body so strongly he could taste it. He felt so buoyed by the news he could have vaulted over the truck to open the door for her. But he didn't. He wanted to shout out loud, but instead he shook her hand to seal the bargain before she got into the truck. Then he just stood there in the street staring as the lights from her truck disappeared.

After she left, he went into the house, turned off the lights and went to bed. But not to sleep. He lay there, staring out the window, his head spinning with the possibilities and problems this move would set in motion.

He'd told her this was a marriage in name only. He'd promised he wouldn't force himself on her. But what if she wanted him as much as he wanted her? He had reason to suspect this was true. Then what? Whatever they did would be legal. It would be moral, too, considering they were both consenting adults. The only thing shady about it was that it wasn't going to last. But no one had to know that. Especially not the bank. Wait a minute. What if Tally told her best friend Suzy and Suzy told her boss.... Jed reached for his bedside phone.

Tally answered on the first ring. "Are you asleep?" he asked.

"No."

"Have you told anyone yet?" he asked.

"Like who?"

"I don't want you to tell anybody *why* we're getting married. You know how it is in Harmony. There are no secrets. And if our friend Dwight hears that it's just a marriage of convenience, that we're doing it to get the loan and then get divorced, then we're not going to get the loan."

"But people are going to wonder..."

"Why you're marrying me? Tell them it's my charm."

"Why *you're* marrying *me*."

"Why would they? You heard my mother, you're one of the best riders in the county."

"That's hardly a reason. If it was, why hasn't anyone else asked me?"

"You told me every eligible bachelor either got married or left town. I came back. You were waiting for me."

"Is that the story?" she asked.

"That's it. You could say we've been engaged all these years. You may not want to admit it, but it's close to the truth."

"It is?"

"You promised to marry me," he said firmly. "Don't deny it. There were witnesses."

He heard her breathe into the phone. Warm summer air drifted in through his window. And hers. He wondered what she wore to bed. An oversize T-shirt and bikini pants? A silky negligee? Something lacy? He ground his back teeth together in frustration.

What was it about this woman that sent his senses reeling? That made him hot and throbbing with unfulfilled need? She was just a ranch hand, his tenant, a high school classmate. Someone he'd barely remembered, hardly given the time of day to. Then why had he promised to marry her in fifteen years? Why had he almost failed calculus?

"All right," she sighed. "But it's not going to be easy."

"No one said marriage was easy," he said. "But we've got some things going for us."

"Such as?"

"We're old friends."

"Friends?"

"Okay, acquaintances. But we've known each other a long time. We come from the same background."

"Hardly. I come from over the hardware store. You come from White Horse Ranch."

"We'll redo the big house," he said as if she hadn't spoken, surprised at his enthusiasm for restoring the old place. The place he could hardly wait to escape from fifteen years ago. A vision of the master bedroom flashed through his mind. The huge four-poster bed where a half dozen marriages had been consummated and a score of Whitmores had been conceived. Would she sleep there with him? An electric jolt of awareness hit him in the groin as he thought of Tally lying in his bed under his sheets, wearing the sheerest of negligees, her unruly curls splayed across his pillow.

Then he thought about the bath. The master bath with a claw-foot tub and a view of the mountains in the distance. Again her image intruded on his thoughts. Tally in the tub, half-covered with soap bubbles, her hair cascading over the edge of the porcelain. Why not? Once they were married anything was possible. He suppressed a gleeful smile of anticipation.

"We need to get started," he said in a sudden businesslike tone.

"Now?" she asked, startled.

"As soon as possible. I'll come by for you tomorrow. Today. First we'll hit the bank, then the county seat, the blood tests, the judge."

"Wait a minute. I've got lessons all day."

"Cancel them. Get rid of the students. Get rid of the animals. From now on you're on the payroll. I need you full-time."

"Wait a minute." Suddenly Tally could see her life as she knew it falling apart. She wasn't really going to be a wife, she was going to be an employee. Employed to be a wife-in-name-only, and a foreman. Her horses and her students and her life didn't count.

"This is a horse farm," she said, sitting up in bed and gripping the receiver tightly in her hand. "These horses are in my care, some of them I've had since their birth, and they need my attention. So do my students. I may be on the payroll, but you don't own me. I need time for myself. For what I do. For what I love."

Jed was silent on the other end. Then he said, "Oh...right."

After she hung up, Tally wondered if he'd heard anything she'd said. He was so full of himself and his plans. To him she was just a warm body to be used to get what he wanted. To achieve his goal. Anything that stood in his way he just brushed aside. She assumed that was how he made the fortune he'd made. That was how everyone who was rich got what they wanted.

Since she was thoroughly awake, and too agitated to go back to sleep, Tally got dressed and went out to the stables. She automatically went through the motions of feeding and brushing her horses, while her mind went over and over their conversation. A cold shaft of fear struck her between her shoulder blades. Fear of change. Fear of disappointment. Fear of Jed Whitmore.

What was she thinking? She couldn't marry Jed. She barely knew him. He barely knew her. The idea was preposterous. If Jed didn't realize it yet, he surely would soon. Marry Jed? It was laughable. What would people say?

She didn't have long to find out. As the sun was rising

over the distant mountains, her friend Suzy pulled up at
the ranch in her vintage station wagon.

"You said you'd call me," Suzy said from the open
doorway to the stable.

Tally dropped a bucket of oats in front of her smallest
colt. "What are you doing up so early?"

"I might ask you the same question."

"Man works from sun to sun, but women's work is
never done," Tally explained, moving from stall to stall
with her sack of feed.

"Speaking of man," Suzy began, perching on a bale
of hay, "when you didn't answer your phone this morning, I got worried. I wondered where you were."

"I was right here."

"What about Jed? What about last night?"

"Last night...last night..." Tally wrinkled her forehead as if she couldn't remember. As if she'd ever forget.

"The reunion...the gym...the music...Jed Whitmore," Suzy prompted.

"Oh, yes. Now I remember."

"And?"

"I gave him a ride home. We went in for coffee."

Suzy got to her feet and strode briskly across the barn
floor, forcing Tally to look her in the eye. "Then what?"

"His mother woke up and came into the kitchen."

"Oh, no."

"Oh, yes."

"What did she say?" Suzy asked.

"She said...she said she thought I'd fit in."

"To what? Her wedding dress, or to their family?"

Tally's hand shook so hard she spilled a pail of water
on the floor and she heaved a huge sigh. "Oh, Suzy, he
wants to marry me. What am I to do?"

Suzy's mouth fell open in surprise. ''Do? The richest, best-looking, sexiest man to ever leave Harmony comes back to claim you. And you're asking me what to do?''

''You don't understand,'' Tally said. She swallowed hard over a lump in her throat, knowing she couldn't, she *couldn't* tell Suzy the truth about *why* Jed wanted to marry her.

''I understand that this is the most romantic thing that's ever happened,'' Suzy said. ''I'll never forget the night he said he'd marry you fifteen years ago. And I never thought he'd do it, until last night. Then I saw the way he was looking at you...and I knew!''

''You knew?'' Tally asked.

''I may not know much, but I know true love when I see it.''

Tally couldn't help shaking her head sadly. Poor romantic Suzy, dreaming of being swept off her feet by Prince Charming, sure that's what had happened to Tally. If she only knew it was all a sham. All a business deal. Jed's words came back to her. ''From now on you're on the payroll.'' She was going to be his employee. Nothing more, nothing less. True love, hah!

''Are you saying you're not in love with Jed?'' Suzy asked as if she'd read Tally's thoughts.

''I can't be in love with someone I don't know. Sure, I may have had a crush on him in high school. Along with every other girl in our class, but how did this teenage infatuation turn into true love without my knowing it?''

''Well, if it hasn't yet, it will. Lots of people fall in love after they get married. In Saudi Arabia, all the marriages are arranged and the divorce rate is zero. Come to think of it, Jed reminds me a little bit of a sheik, too.''

''Well, he isn't. He's a businessman. And this is Harmony, not Arabia. We don't arrange marriages here, because it doesn't work. People here fall in love and then get married."

Suzy let this information sink in before she walked backward to the bale of hay and sat down again. "So, what are you going to do?"

"She's going to marry me," Jed said, suddenly appearing from around the corner of the barn.

Tally gripped the support beam on Gypsy's stall to steady her trembling hands and keep from falling apart at the seams. She didn't expect to see him so soon. Were his electric blue eyes just a shade heavy-lidded from lack of sleep? If so, his smile was just as seductive as he stood there, one arm braced against the weathered wood, looking at her. He was gorgeous, no getting around it, right out of a magazine with his sun-bleached hair and expensive casual shirt and jeans. She glanced down at the rip in the knee of her own jeans and the smear of dirt on her shirt and realized she must look like hell, with her bleary eyes and snarled hair.

She wondered how long Jed had been outside the barn and how much he'd heard. She'd prefer Jed didn't know she'd had a crush on him in high school. Whatever he'd heard, he couldn't accuse her of telling Suzy the truth: that they were getting married to fulfill the bank's loan requirements.

"Congratulations," Suzy said leaping to her feet to shake Jed's hand. "Am I the first to know?"

"The second. I told my mother this morning."

Tally gave Jed an inquisitive look.

"She's delighted, of course."

"Of course," Tally murmured.

"So you two have been..." Suzy began.

"Engaged all this time," Jed filled in.

"That was a *long* engagement," Suzy remarked, looking from Jed to Tally and back again.

"We wanted to be sure," Jed said, walking through loose straw to put his arm around Tally. "Didn't we?" he asked looking down at her with a fathomless look in his eyes.

Tally froze. Suzy wasn't fooled. Nobody else would be, either. As soon as Suzy finally left, after asking to be a bridesmaid, Tally pulled away from Jed.

"You're overdoing it," she said, backing up against Gypsy's stall. "Nobody's engaged for fifteen years."

"*We* were," he said.

"All right, we were," she said suddenly weary of the game. "But nobody's going to believe it."

"They might if you stopped looking at me like I was Count Dracula."

"I'm sorry." She pressed her fingers against her temples to stop the throbbing that had started early that morning.

Jed reached for her hands and took them in his. His touch sent shivers running up and down her spine. She didn't dare meet his gaze. Afraid to let him see how much he affected her. Let him think what he wanted. That she thought he was repellent. It was better than him knowing the truth. She was dangerously, powerfully attracted to him. Always had been and, God help her, always would be.

"Tally," he said, his voice muted by the cavernous barn. "If you want to back out of this, say so."

"If I say no, what will you do?" she asked.

"Marry someone else, I suppose."

The sweet smell of hay filled the air and mingled with the clean, masculine scent of Jed Whitmore. Shafts of early-morning sunlight shone through the cracks in the roof. The peaceful scene was a vivid contrast to the wild beating of her heart.

Say no and he would disappear from her life. As fast as he'd appeared. No more Jed, no more barn, no home for her horses, no home for herself. Starting over, somewhere else. Say no and Jed would marry someone else. Someone more suited than she to be a Whitmore.

"Someone more suited to life at White Horse Ranch," she murmured. The chill that enveloped her heart contrasted with the warmth of his hands holding hers. Her heart thumped so loudly in her chest he must hear it. He must know how she felt about him. How just his glance or his touch could throw her heart into overdrive.

"No one's more suited to life at the ranch than you," he said evenly, matter-of-factly. He was so cool, so businesslike.

"You amaze me, you know," she said, withdrawing her hands from his and fiddling with Gypsy's harness. "We're talking about marriage, but to you it's like a business deal. I know...I know. It *is* a business deal. But...I always thought when I got married, *if* I got married..."

"What...? Oh, I get it. This is not romantic enough for you. You want romance? I'll give you romance... come here."

He reached for her and hauled her into his arms. Something he'd wanted to do the minute he saw her this morning, in her rumpled shirt, her tousled hair and her fresh scrubbed face, devoid of makeup, devoid of artifice. She was so natural, so real, oozing good health and energy, so much her own person. Compared to all the women he'd known since he left Harmony, and there had been many, she stood out from the crowd like a proud Thoroughbred.

She wanted romance. He'd show her romance. A hug, a squeeze, a tender kiss or two. But what had started as a joke turned into something else entirely. The tender kiss turned passionate as their mouths fused. She tasted like sunshine and summer, and he couldn't get enough of her. Warmth became heat and heat turned into fire as his tongue plunged between her parted lips to plunder, explore and excite.

Throbbing with need, he backed her into the smooth old boards that separated the barn from the stable. A throaty moan escaped Tally's lips as she frantically gripped fistfuls of his shirt with both hands.

Cupping her firm, denim-covered bottom Jed brought her close, closer until she fitted tight against his aching arousal. A horse nickered softly in the background, while his heart pounded loudly in his ears. He kissed her again and again. Her every sigh, every soft moan fueled his passion like oil on flames until he was at the brink of spontaneous combustion. In another minute he'd be dragging her up to the loft to rip her clothes off. Some small remnant of reason told him the least he could do was wait till after the wedding.

He moved his hands to rest on her hips, and with every ounce of willpower he possessed, he broke the kiss. She wiped her red, swollen lips with the back of one hand. With the other hand she steadied herself and looked up at him, her silver-gray eyes cloudy and confused.

"What happened?" she asked.

"Must be something in the air," he said, unwilling to confess he'd been swept away in a firestorm. No way did he want to get emotionally involved with somebody from Harmony, no matter how good a rider or how deliciously sexy she was. Theirs was going to be a marriage of convenience. Beneficial to both of them. A marriage with beginning, middle and end. There was no harm in enjoying the fringe benefits of marriage while they were at it, as long as nobody got hurt and nobody had any expectations other than those stated in the agreement. Which reminded him…

"Let's get going," he said, dropping his hands from her waist with a sharp twinge of regret.

She looked down at her faded denims. "Not yet. Not like this. I've got things to do, calls to make, then I have to clean up. You'll have to wait."

Instead of just waiting, he helped her. While she showered and dressed, he dumped hay into feed bins. He was surprised at how satisfying the work was. He remembered it as being pure drudgery. But he felt useful and content at some elemental level that was unfamiliar to him.

When she finally got into his car, wearing her bank dress, he drew in a sharp breath, remembering that day they'd sat in Dwight's office asking for the loan. Not the first time he'd been aware of her as a desirable woman, but a memorable moment, anyway. Today he would keep his cool, having lost it once today already. It should be easy.

Nothing was easy. He should have known better than to think he could control his libido with her arm brushing his in Dwight's office. With her hair filling his senses with its soft fragrance, the sight of her firm, upturned breasts outlined under her flowered dress. All reminding him of how her hot lips felt against his, how her pliant body pressed against his that morning. All reminding him that the sooner they got married, the sooner they could consummate their union.

They signed papers, they took blood tests, they talked to architects, contractors and lenders. They ended the day at his mother's house to talk about the wedding.

Tally wiped her damp palms against the flowered fabric of her skirt as Jed opened the heavy oak door to his mother's elegant town house. If Jed was as nervous as she was, he didn't show it. But why should he be? He'd always pushed the envelope farther than anyone else. Marrying Tally, while not the most sensible thing he'd ever done, was probably not the most outrageous, either. And his mother's indulgence had extended all the way to Tally, at least last night it had. Still...

Mrs. Whitmore greeted her just as warmly from her restored eighteenth-century desk in the living room, causing the butterflies in Tally's stomach to cease their frantic activity.

"Good news," Jed announced. "Tally's going to marry me."

Mrs. Whitmore rose from her chair and hugged Tally with genuine enthusiasm. Then she stood back and looked from Jed to Tally. "I'm delighted. Really I am. It's sudden, but in a way, it's not sudden at all. You've known each other forever. And anyone can see you're in love."

Jed cleared his throat and went to the kitchen to get drinks.

"Champagne," his mother called as he disappeared down the hallway. Then Mrs. Whitmore drew Tally to the natural linen-covered couch and sat beside her. "In the absence of your family," she said tactfully refraining from saying, *in the absence of your family's money*, "I'd like to give the wedding. If that's all right with you."

Tally nodded gratefully. "That would be lovely. The only thing is…Jed wants it right away."

Mrs. Whitmore smiled understandingly. "I'm sure he does. But it takes time to plan a wedding. And since it's the only one I'm likely to plan, I want to do it right." She leaned forward and clasped Tally's hands in hers. "I am happy about this, very happy. I had begun to think…as every mother does, that I might not live to see any grandchildren."

Tally bit her lip to stop the rush of tears to her eyes. How could she let this generous woman think their union would produce the grandchildren she wanted so much. Without thinking she jumped to her feet. "I—I'd better go help Jed," she blurted.

She burst into the kitchen just as Jed was opening a bottle of champagne. The cork popped into the air at the same time that Tally's temper exploded.

"You've got to tell her the truth. It isn't fair. She thinks it's going to last…she thinks she's going to have grandchildren!"

Jed set the bottle on the counter and patted Tally on the back. "It's okay. She's been talking about grandchildren for years. She'll be talking about them for years to come. That kind of disappointment she can take. What she can't take is thinking I need money. She'd want to give it to me or lend it to me herself. I can't let her do that. Do you understand?" he asked, looking into Tally's eyes, his hand on her shoulder.

"I guess so," she said dubiously. But what she didn't understand was who Jed was protecting. Who would be hurt most by his telling the truth? Jed, by admitting he needed money, or his mother by learning he wasn't as successful as she'd thought? "But she's so…so nice," Tally protested.

"Of course she's nice. She's my mother."

"I see. It's inherited," Tally said dryly.

Jed grinned and they went back to the living room and toasted their engagement. But Tally felt guilty every time she looked at his mother. Every time his mother looked at her with that gleam in her eyes. The gleam that said she saw her dream of having grandchildren about to come true. The gleam that scared Tally half to death.

# Chapter Five

It was a beautiful wedding. Everyone said so. The first wedding at White Horse Ranch in thirty-five years. The bride arrived at the front steps of the old house in the traditional palomino-drawn carriage. Wearing the traditional ivory wedding gown. The whole town was invited to the reception held under a huge tent on the front lawn. Another tradition.

As in small towns everywhere, where there's an unlikely match and a wedding is thrown together hastily, rumors flew.

"A shotgun wedding, no doubt about it."

"The Whitmores tried to buy her off, but she wouldn't go."

"A Cinderella story. A beautiful bride and a happy ending."

"Jed hasn't changed. He always gets what he wants."

"I give it six months."

"Six weeks."

Tally, sitting behind a giant floral arrangement of pink

roses and lavender orchids, with her shoes off and a glass of champagne in her hand, heard them all. Her face flushed the color of the roses while she tried to decide whether to laugh or cry. It was that kind of day. With the minister, the friends and relatives all wondering how, where and why.

And then there was Jed. Waiting at the white-latticed gazebo on the lawn as she marched reluctantly toward him. Suzy insisted Tally had floated across the grass, but all Tally could remember was that her feet felt like lead and that Jed's eyes never left her face, watching her anxiously as if she might take a wrong turn and end up at the stables instead.

Frauds. Both of them. Promising to love, honor and obey till death do them part. By all rights they should have been struck by lightning. But they weren't. She was hiding behind the flowers and Jed was circulating. While he was talking with his business associates, he spotted her.

"Tally, come and meet some people," he ordered.

She slipped her shoes back onto her sore feet, set her glass down and pasted a smile on her face.

"Jed's the last person we thought would ever get married," his friend Steve said when she joined them.

*And I'm the last person you thought he'd marry,* she thought. "Really?" she said brightly. "Why is that?"

"Well, frankly he was a moving target. Never stayed in one place long enough for any woman to sink her claws into him. Not that you—"

Jed took Tally's hand in his and laced his fingers through hers. Her smile slipped a notch. It was all she could do to keep from yanking her hand away. To keep from shouting, *Can't you see it's not for real. It's all phony.*